All over the country children go to stay with step-parents, stepbrothers and stepsisters at the weekends. It's just like an endless chain. A step-chain. *Parents Behaving Badly* is the sixth link in this step-chain.

I'm Hannah, and right now I'm sick of my parents. It's not fair that everyone else is being dragged into their problems. My stepsister, who's also my best friend, has turned her back on me. My brother's being a complete pain. Somehow I've got to sort this out, because if these pathetic grown-ups don't get their act together, my life is going to be in ruins . . .

Collect the links in the step-chain! You never know who you'll meet on the way...

 1 One Mum Too Many! – Sarah

 2 You Can't Fancy Your Stepsister – Ollie

 3 She's No Angel – Lissie

 4 Too Good To Be True – Becca

 5 Get Me Out Of Here – Ed

 6 Parents Behaving Badly – Hannah

Coming soon

 7 Don't Tell Mum – Bethany

 8 Losing My Identity – Ryan

 9 Secrets And Lies – Katie

PARENTS BEHAVING BADLY

Ann Bryant

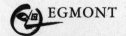

EGMONT

First published in Great Britain 2002
by Egmont Books Limited
239 Kensington High Street
London W8 6SA

Series editor: Anne Finnis

ISBN 0 7497 4845 1

1 3 5 7 9 10 8 6 4 2

Typeset by Avon Dataset Ltd, Bidford on Avon, B50 4JH
(www.avondataset.co.uk)
Printed and bound in Great Britain by
Cox & Wyman Ltd, Reading, Berkshire

CONTENTS

1	Families out of step	1
2	Mission unite	16
3	After tomorrow	24
4	Telling Rachel	35
5	The bond	50
6	Happy families	60
7	Sorted	69
8	The kitchen – before and after	79
9	Sussing Craig	91
10	The rocket joke	104
11	Unravelling	109
12	Operation Tina	121
13	Accounts	133
14	Esther	143
15	The million dollar question	152

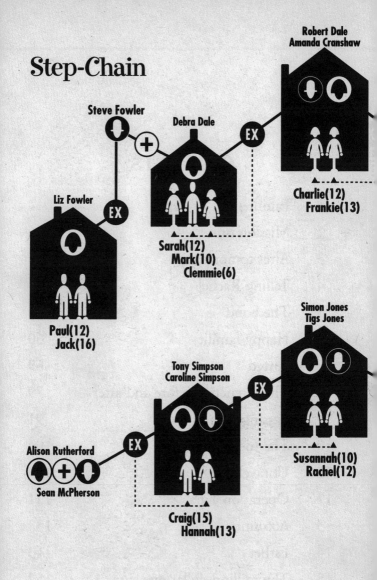

Step-Chain

Steve Fowler

Debra Dale

Robert Dale
Amanda Cranshaw

Liz Fowler

Charlie(12)
Frankie(13)

Sarah(12)
Mark(10)
Clemmie(6)

Paul(12)
Jack(16)

Simon Jones
Tigs Jones

Tony Simpson
Caroline Simpson

Alison Rutherford

Sean McPherson

Susannah(10)
Rachel(12)

Craig(15)
Hannah(13)

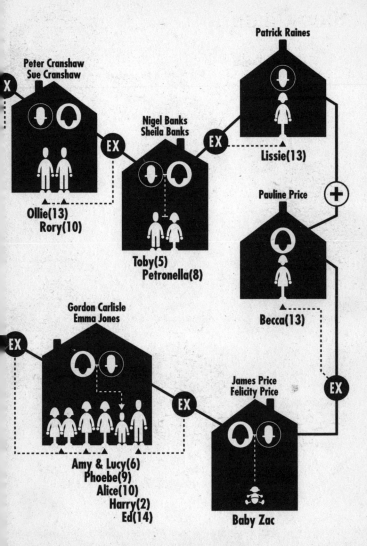

Read on to discover all the links . . .

1 FAMILIES OUT OF STEP

'OK, pipe down, you lot!' said Mrs Waghorn, standing up at the front of the coach for about the tenth time.

'It's because we're in a good mood, Miss,' said Chris Carter, the year nine mouthpiece.

The boys at the back all jeered, but jokingly. They liked Chris. He always spoke his mind.

'Yeah, you should be flattered, Miss. It's you who's put us in a good mood.'

'Just sit down and be quiet for the last ten minutes. You say I've made *you* happy – well now make *me* happy.'

We were on our way back from a really brilliant play. It was a school outing for years eight and nine. The theatre company we'd just seen only ever did performances for schools, specially to help students understand Shakespeare. Even the loud boys like Chris and Sean really enjoyed it.

I loved the whole outing because my stepsister Rachel and I got to sit next to each other on the coach there and back. She's in year eight and I'm in year nine, though our birthdays aren't that far apart.

'Oi, Hannah! Isn't that your brother?' Chris asked me.

The coach had stopped at the lights. I rubbed the window with my hand because it was all steamed up. Craig was walking on the opposite pavement a little way ahead.

Rachel leaned over me and peered out too. 'He's right, it *is* Craig. What's he doing, Han?'

'Haven't a clue,' I said.

She lowered her voice. 'Is he still acting strange?' I nodded. 'Poor Han.'

'Poor, pathetic parents more like.'

'What are you two whispering about?' asked Katie, one of my best friends in year nine, draping her arms over our seat from behind.

'Nothing interesting,' said Rachel.

We'd pulled away from the lights and were catching up with Craig. I knocked on the window to attract his attention, then half the coach joined in.

'Craig!' called Naomi, my other best friend in year nine.

'Girls at the back, less noise!' said Mrs Waghorn. 'You're still representing the school you know.'

'Yes, shut up, girls!' said Chris, putting on a teacherly voice. 'Learn some decent manners, like us boys!'

All the boys laughed, and Craig happened to glance up at that moment and catch sight of me. He hardly smiled at all.

'Your brother doesn't look too happy. Have you been upsetting him, Hannah?' asked Chris, grinning all over his face.

'Shut up, Chris,' said Rachel. 'You wouldn't understand a family problem if you had three years' private coaching on the subject.'

I knew Rachel would tell Chris where to get off. We always stick up for each other because we're not only stepsisters, we're best friends too.

As we approached school, people started dragging their bags down from the luggage racks.

'Who's picking you up?' Rachel asked me, her eyes all sympathetic.

'Mum.'

'What time's Dad coming home?'

'Usual, I think.'

'Give me a ring if things get bad.'

'Yeah. Thanks.'

Rachel is the only person who understands

what it's like at home these days. We've known each other since she was six and I was seven. That's when her dad (Tony) left her mum, because he'd fallen in love with *my* mum. Mum and Craig and I had been living on our own for about a year before that, because my real dad left Mum and went back to Scotland where he grew up.

It seems so long ago now, but Dad had been spending more and more time in Scotland on business, and finally he decided to move up there for good. Mum didn't want to go with him and because I was quite young at the time I couldn't work out why. It turned out that he had a girlfriend. It was horrible just before he went, but it was a relief once he'd actually gone. Mum seemed happier, and I didn't miss him because I'd got so used to him being away.

Lots of people think it's weird because Rachel's dad is my stepdad, but Rachel and I are really fine with it. We've both got a mum and a stepdad to live with, and it makes things even better that we're stepsisters.

The problem is our mums. They don't speak to each other if they can possibly help it, because they can't stand each other. It can be quite embarrassing and awkward for Rachel and me at times, even though we're used to it now. Sometimes we feel like wringing our mothers' necks and telling them to grow up, but we've found it's best not to say anything if we don't want to get screamed at.

When Tony first moved in with us, there were massive arguments on the phone between Rachel's mum and him. Since then each set of parents has tried to pretend the other doesn't exist. Our mums used to try and keep us apart. Rachel's mum, Tigs, didn't want her daughter in the same house as Mum because she was so jealous of her, especially when Mum and Tony got married. And Mum's never been happy about Tigs and her new husband, Simon, living so close. She hates it when Tony has to get in touch with Tigs about anything to do with Rachel or Susannah, his other daughter. I can tell she wishes that Rachel and I weren't best friends, but she knows after all these years that she can't stop us.

But these last few months everything's worse than ever because things have started to go wrong between Mum and Tony. If Tony ever left us I'd be gutted because he's just like a proper dad to me and Craig. But the arguments between him and Mum are getting worse and worse. Sometimes it's like they hate each other's guts.

The coach swung into the school car park, and I saw Mum's car straight away. When I looked carefully I could also see her face. She was pressing her fingertips against her lips and staring straight ahead blankly. This was her usual expression these days.

I said 'bye to everyone then got in the car.

'So? Was it good?'

Mum's face came to life with a big bright smile. It reminded me of the moment when the Prince kisses the Sleeping Beauty and she wakes up.

'Yeah, excellent. Even Chris Carter liked it.'

'Wow! It *must* have been good!'

'I'm starving.'

'Spag bol tonight.'

I wanted to know if Tony was going to eat with us, or if he was going to be late back from work again, but I didn't dare even say his name. It would only make Mum go tense and tight-lipped. That's how all the bad stuff had started with my real dad. Even when he wasn't actually away, he kept on being late home from work.

To make matters worse, Craig is changing. He and I used to talk to each other about all sorts of stuff, but if I try to talk now, he just grunts out a reply. So I've given up. I know he hates it when Mum and Tony are arguing, but it's almost as though he's taking it out on me.

Tony wasn't late, but we didn't all eat together. He and Craig ate their spag bol in the kitchen, while Mum and I went into the living-room and watched telly. Craig acts practically normally when he and Tony are together, as long as Mum isn't in the same room. They laugh and joke as though they don't have a care in the world. But the moment Mum comes in, Craig goes all sullen and bolshie.

'I'll take the plates through,' I said during the adverts.

Mum just nodded. Her face had got that marble look on it, and I wondered if she'd actually taken in any of the programme, or if she'd just been staring at the screen, wrapped up in her own thoughts, seeing nothing except the pictures inside her head.

In the kitchen Craig and Tony were playing a

game on their mobile phones. Tony didn't even know he'd got any games on his phone until Craig showed him. And now he's obsessed. The two of them sit there, staring at their tiny little screens and trying to get a higher score than the other one.

'Can you show me how to play?' I asked, seeing them having such a good time.

'Ssh!' said Craig, his thumbs tapping away.

I loaded the plates in the dishwasher while they finished.

'Top score! Six hundred!' yelled Tony, as his phone rang a bright little tune to celebrate. 'What did you get?'

'Four hundred and fifty,' said Craig, looking hacked off.

'That makes it three–two, I believe!'

'Oh thanks, Hannah,' Craig said sarcastically to me.

'What? I didn't do anything.'

'You made me lose concentration.'

'So-*rry*!'

'Yeah, right. Tony's the overall winner now.'

'Let me have a go, Craig,' I begged.

'You'll never beat the champ,' swaggered Tony.

And that was when Mum came into the kitchen.

Something instantly changed. We might as well have pumped in ice-cold air. It was horrible, just like it always is these days.

'I'm off to Josh's,' said Craig, scraping his chair as he got up.

'See you later,' said Tony, trying to keep his voice light, but failing.

Craig grunted. He's nearly sixteen. He can escape – lucky thing. I'm only thirteen, so it's a bit more difficult.

'I've got homework,' I mumbled as I got up.

I waited outside the kitchen door to hear what they'd say, even though I knew it was a stupid thing to do because I'd only get upset.

It's horrible when you hear two people you love having an argument.

'They both take off like frightened animals the moment we're in the same room,' said Mum.

She sounded tired and sad.

Then Tony spoke. 'We were perfectly OK till *you* came in.'

'Are you saying it's my fault?'

'I'm just saying we were perfectly OK till you came in.'

The phone rang. Tony answered it.

'Hello . . . Hello love. How're you doing?'

It was either Susannah or Rachel. These days, apart from me, the only people he talks to in that affectionate tone of voice are his real daughters. Let's hope it was Rachel. I felt like a chat.

Hang on a sec . . . what am I saying? If it is Rachel, I'm going to get caught eavesdropping outside the kitchen door any second!

I rushed upstairs in the nick of time.

'Hannah . . . Phone. It's Rachel,' called Tony. 'I'll take it up here.'

Getting the phone from Mum and Tony's room, I went into my own room and lay on the bed.

'Hi, Han. Guess what – Mum's found this conditioner that's supposed to straighten your hair. You leave it on for twenty minutes and keep combing and combing your hair the whole time it's on. I'm doing it now!'

It was always great to hear Rachel's voice. Even when I've been with her loads during the day, like today, we never run out of things to say. Rachel's got a thing about her curly hair. She says she'd give anything to have straight hair like mine. But the trouble with mine is that it's too fine. The only reason I've grown it nearly to my waist is because if I had it any shorter, it would seem like I'd hardly *got* any hair.

'Sounds great, Rach! Can't wait to see it tomorrow!'

'Are things really bad, Han?'

I didn't think I'd shown my feelings in my voice, but Rachel knows me so well, she can tell if anything's wrong, even when I try to cover it up.

'You're not kidding. Mum walked into the room and the atmosphere froze over, then when they tried speaking to each other it was an instant argument. Can you come round?'

'I'll ask. Expect me if you see me.'

'OK.'

We often use those words – *expect me if you see me* – at the end of our phone calls. Basically it means *I'll be allowed to come over if Mum's in a good mood*. I know it's strange that I live with Rachel's dad, but most of the time it feels completely normal. Just occasionally it hits me though – like now. My best friend is sympathising with me about *my* problem living with *her* dad. How weird is *that?* I know she's got her own stepdad, but in a way that just makes it even stranger, because *his* children live with someone else's dad . . . And so it goes on. It's one great long chain of families, all out of step with each other.

2 MISSION UNITE

There was a knock on the front door. Mum was in the kitchen.

'I'll get it.'

I belted down the stairs. She beat me to it.

'Oh – hello, Rachel.'

Rachel's hair looked exactly the same as ever. She must have seen me looking at it.

'Didn't work,' she said.

I could tell by the look on Mum's face that she wasn't too pleased to see Rachel. She doesn't usually let it show, but I suppose right now, anything to do with Tony – even his daughter –

gets to her. She went back into the kitchen and started clearing things from the table as though her life depended on it – another clue that she wasn't particularly impressed. I knew Rachel wouldn't take it personally. She'd just assume it was Mum's general bad mood.

We went up to my room.

'Only eighteen days to go!' Rachel said. I pretended not to understand. 'Until I'm a teenager . . .'

'I know really.' I grinned at her. 'Has your mum agreed to a party yet?'

'No, she's still saying I'm not allowed because of the house being such a tip at the moment with the re-wiring. I was thinking of asking Dad if I could have one here, but that's probably not the greatest idea in the world, is it?'

'Not right now, no,' I said, feeling sorry for her.

'Where *is* Dad, anyway?'

'Gone out to the pub, I guess. I heard the

door slam when I was on the phone to you. I didn't dare ask Mum. You've only got to mention his name and her face goes all pinched and horrible.'

'Do you think they might . . . you know . . .'

'What?' My heart was beating faster. Neither of us had ever mentioned the 'D' word, and I didn't want her to say it now. It was an unbearable thought.

'Split up.'

At least she didn't say divorce.

'No.'

'It'd be terrible if they did . . .'

'They won't.'

'. . . because we wouldn't be stepsisters any more, would we?'

For the first time it hit me.

'I – I don't think they'll split up,' I said, trying to sound confident. Rachel's face was all white. Mine was probably the same. I didn't feel confident, I felt terrified.

'We're just going to have to make sure they don't,' she said firmly. 'I'll come round here as often as possible, and the moment there's any sign of an argument starting, we'll stop it.'

'OK,' I said, wondering how on earth we were supposed to do that. Rachel hadn't heard Mum and Tony going at it hammer and tongs, like I had.

'The trouble is,' I said carefully, because I didn't want to put her off *too* much, 'sometimes it's so bad you just want to walk away. That's what Craig does. Well, not exactly *walk* away, more *crash* away.'

'What do you mean?'

'He gets as angry as Mum and Tony do. Like last night – he kicked a chair over and slammed the door so hard the handle fell off.'

Bang on cue, we both heard a key turning in the front door.

'Is that Craig?' Rachel was whispering, as though she was scared in case he came crashing upstairs and kicked *my* door in.

'No, it'll be Tony. He can't have gone to the pub after all. Craig usually comes in through the back.'

'Right, let's get started,' said Rachel, her eyes all big.

'Yeah. Mission Unite!' I announced.

'Mission Unite!' said Rachel, punching her fist in the air. Then we both rushed out of the bedroom before we could change our minds.

'Hiya, Rach!' said Tony, as we came downstairs. 'What are you two up to?'

'Hi, Dad! Hannah and I were just talking about my birthday. Mum says I can't have a party at home because of all the re-wiring mess. Any chance I can have one here instead?'

'Well . . . I hadn't really thought about it . . .'

Mum came out of the kitchen with a stony face.

'Not sure about what?'

'I was just talking to the girls,' said Tony,

without even bothering to look at Mum.

'If you're discussing birthday parties in this house, I think it does concern me ever so slightly,' said Mum in her most sarcastic voice.

Rachel and I looked at each other. An argument had already started. We had to try and stop it before it turned into a shouting match. Rachel's eyes were bigger than usual. Unless you've actually witnessed an argument between Mum and Tony, you can't imagine how bad they are.

'If Rachel and I organise everything, can we have the party here, Mum?'

'So you're going to drive to Tesco and do all the shopping, are you?'

I hated the sarcastic way Mum was talking.

'*I'll* do the shopping if it's that much of a problem,' said Tony very sharply.

'Yeah? And the cooking? And clean the house before and after, and supervise all through? Doesn't sound like your usual style, Tony.'

Rachel's eyes were nearly popping out of her head. 'It doesn't matter,' she said softly. 'I won't have a party.'

'See what you've done now,' Tony snarled.

'That's right, blame it on me!' said Mum, raising her voice.

Then she stomped back into the kitchen, slamming the door behind her. Tony looked down at the carpet with his mouth in a tight, thin line. Rachel and I stood perfectly still, not even daring to look at each other.

A few seconds later Tony gave us both a sort of sad smile. Then his expression changed to one of determination. 'If you want a party, love, I don't see why you shouldn't have one.'

'We don't want to make Mum . . . cross,' I said carefully.

'Just leave it to me,' said Tony. He was trying to smile, but it didn't look very genuine. 'We'll talk about it tomorrow, OK?'

Then he went into the living-room and

Rachel and I heard the television coming on before we crept back upstairs.

'Mission Unite wasn't exactly the success story of the year, was it?' Rachel said flatly. She looked sad.

But I felt furious. 'Pathetic grown-ups. They ought to get their acts together!'

3 AFTER TOMORROW

'Craig didn't say anything to you about where he was going, did he?' Mum asked me when I was about to go to bed. 'Only I've tried his mobile but it's switched off.'

'No.'

'I'll ask Tony . . .' I held my breath as she opened the living-room door. 'Did Craig tell you where he was going tonight?' I heard her ask him in a very controlled voice.

Tony jumped down her throat. 'No, he didn't. He was in a bit of a hurry to get out of the house, if you remember.'

'I was only asking.'

Mum slammed the door, then stood there biting her lip, with hunched shoulders and a deep frown.

'He'll be in soon. He's never stayed out all night before,' I said to try and cheer her up.

She had tears in her eyes as she said goodnight to me.

It was about two hours later when I heard him come in. The house was in darkness. I sat up in bed and listened.

The sound of a chair crashing to the floor in the kitchen made me jump, because the rest of the house was so silent. Then I heard Craig swear. He must have been in the hall. His footsteps were heavy on the stairs, as though he wasn't trying to be quiet at all. There was something else odd about his footsteps, but I couldn't think what it was.

I heard first the bathroom light click on, then

the taps being turned full on. And the next thing, shattering the last bit of peace, was Tony's angry voice outside the bathroom door.

'How dare you come in at this hour and wake up the whole household!'

'Well, if the "household", as you call it, wasn't awake before, it certainly will be now it's heard your dulcet tones,' Craig said, slurring his words.

And that's when I realised what was odd about the way he'd come upstairs. His footsteps were uneven because he was drunk. Tony was going to go mad.

'You've been drinking, you stupid idiot!' Tony snarled.

I heard Mum come across the landing. 'Leave it, Tony. We'll talk in the morning. At least he's here,' she said, her voice all shaky with emotion.

'No, I will not leave it!' he shouted.

Craig laughed – a horrible, bitter, fake laugh.

'Here we go!' he said in a falsely cheerful

voice. 'I knew there was some reason why I would have been better off staying out all night. Must remember next time. Now 'scuse me, you two love birds – some of us have got to get some kip.'

I buried my head under the duvet, put my fingers in my ears and counted to fifty. My eyes were tight shut too, just in case the heavy duvet and the closed bedroom door weren't enough to block out the horrible turmoil that raged on the landing. When I emerged from my hiding place the house was quiet apart from a few muffled taps and scrapes from Craig's room.

'It was awful,' I told Rachel at break time the next day.

'Poor you,' she said. 'Things are getting worse, aren't they?' I nodded. 'I'd definitely better forget about my party then. It's no big deal anyway.'

'No – I reckon we should stick out for a party, because Mum and Tony will both have to be there and they won't be able to argue in front of all the guests. If there's a good atmosphere, they might even enjoy themselves. It's all part of Mission Unite.'

'But how are we going to get your mum to agree to the party in the first place?'

'I'll talk to her. She'll be fine.'

I wasn't at all sure about that, but I could only try.

'I bet she and Dad don't buy me a joint present this year, like they usually do.'

'Never mind – two presents are better than one,' I said, grinning at her.

'Oi!'

'Josh's here,' Rachel said, nodding towards the classroom door, where Josh Rogers, one of Craig's friends, was trying to attract my attention.

'Where's Craig?'

'Somewhere around.' *Why was he asking* me?

'No, he's not. Must be bunking. S'OK.'

And he disappeared.

'Craig's bunking off!' I breathed, as I stared into space, my heart banging against my ribs. 'Mum and Tony'll go spare.'

'Was everything back to normal when you got up this morning?' Rachel asked me, wide eyed.

'Well, Craig wasn't talking to Mum or Tony, and Mum and Tony weren't talking to each other, but I suppose that's pretty normal nowadays.'

'Mum, you know Rachel's birthday,' I said that evening before Tony came back from work, when Mum, Craig and I were in the kitchen.

Mum interrupted me in a trembly loud voice, as though she was at the end of her tether. 'Please don't ask me if she can have a party here, Hannah.' Then she came and sat at the table and took a deep breath. 'Look, there's something I want to say to you both.'

Craig sank lower in his chair and carried on reading the newspaper. 'You and Tony are splitting up. Right?' he said in a hard voice.

I gasped. Mum kind of straightened up and shot glances all over the kitchen as though she was looking for the culprit who'd already revealed her news to us. Then she began gabbling. 'I – I'm sorry that you've both had to put up with so much . . . so many . . . rows and things, but it'll be better from now on.'

'Starting when?' asked Craig.

He still hadn't taken his eyes off the newspaper.

Mum looked panicky. I don't think she'd expected Craig to react like this.

'Let's wait till Tony gets back and he can tell you.'

'So who's moving out?' Craig went on, practically drawling. 'Apart from me?'

'What do you mean apart from you?' I asked, feeling terrified inside. It was as though I was watching a computer screen with pages and pages of my homework on it, and it was under attack from a virus and all the words were falling off the screen into nowhere, never to be seen again. Only it was much worse than that because it wasn't words that were disappearing, it was my family, my past – all the good times we'd had in the last five years since Mum and Tony and Craig and I had lived here together.

Tears were gathering in my eyes and there was nothing I could do about it. Mum leaned over and gave me a hug. Craig got up, his chair scraping as usual, and stood over Mum.

'Come on, tell us, then. You can't make things any worse than they are already.'

'I know you're angry, Craig, but please try to be calm –'

'Oh yeah, that's rich, coming from you.' He sneered and sat down again, then flicked the newspaper page over roughly and pored over it.

I sniffed and tried not to cry.

'You're only upsetting Hannah, Craig.'

'Oh! *I'm* upsetting Hannah, am I?' said Craig, poking his head forwards in a horrible gesture that he never usually did. 'Funny, I could have sworn it was *you* upsetting her.'

The back door opened and in came Tony. He looked at me, then at Craig and finally at Mum.

'They know,' Mum said softly over my head.

Tony's face looked as though the muscles didn't work.

'Oh great,' he said. 'Thanks for waiting for me.'

'I couldn't wait any longer,' Mum shouted. 'Anyway, Craig already guessed!'

And suddenly I'd had enough. I pulled away from Mum and looked from her to Tony. Then, from the pit of my stomach, an enormous torrent of angry words surged up and out of my mouth.

'Shut up!' I screamed. 'You make me sick, both of you. You ought to think about Craig and me a bit more. We hate living in this horrible atmosphere. Why can't you just make yourselves stop arguing all the time instead of making our family split up?' I knew I must have sounded about five and a half, but I couldn't help it. Mum looked as though I'd punched her in the stomach. She put her arm out to me, but I was too cross to be close to her. In fact I wanted to hurt her. Tony's head was down, and Craig was watching me without any expression on his face. 'And Rachel's had enough as well!'

The moment the words were out of my mouth, I realised I'd got it wrong. Mum dropped her arm, and her face masked over with irritation.

'What's Rachel got to do with anything? You can't make me out to be responsible for her feelings too.'

'Don't talk about my daughter like that,' said Tony, looking daggers at Mum. 'She does have feelings, you know.'

'Oh, spare me,' said Craig, getting up abruptly and leaving the kitchen by the hall door.

'Just tell me what's going to happen to me and Craig,' I said through tears.

'I'm moving into rented accommodation for a while,' said Tony quietly. 'I won't be far away. I'll still be able to see you . . . lots. Try not to worry about Rachel – she's got her mum and Simon.' Tony was near to tears himself. 'And you'll still have me, even though I won't be right here . . .'

Mum was sucking her lips in.

'When are you moving out?' I asked Tony in a whisper.

'This weekend.'

That's tomorrow. Nothing's going to be the same after tomorrow.

4 TELLING RACHEL

That weekend was the worst weekend of my life. It turned out that Rachel had to go and visit her uncle Keith, and Mum said I had to come with her to Granny's, which is nearly two hours away by car. Craig stayed at Josh's house. Mum obviously didn't want me around while Tony was getting his things together and going. And I didn't want to be around, either. I wondered if Tony had asked Rachel's mum to arrange a visit to Uncle Keith's, so Rachel and I couldn't get together and wind each other up.

It's not that I don't like being at Granny's,

because I do. She was in an extra good mood, making everything as much fun as possible for us. But that only made everything seem worse. I felt like a little kid having to be distracted from something by the adults.

When I came back from buying a Sunday paper for Mum, I walked in on Gran and Mum having a heart to heart. They stopped abruptly when they saw me, but I'd already overheard Gran saying, 'Well, you'd certainly be right away from Tony if you did,' and that was when I first had the horrible thought that Mum might be intending to move.

Moving anywhere would be awful, but 'right away from Tony' would be the worst thing I could imagine because I'd miss him terribly. And then there was Rachel. I couldn't bear to be parted from my stepsister. I was so cross I felt like going mad at Mum, but there was still a chance that I might have got it wrong and they weren't talking about that at all. The last thing I wanted to do was to put ideas in Mum's head. So I decided to keep quiet and pretend I'd never heard a word of their conversation.

When we came back on Sunday night I felt empty and hopeless inside. It wasn't that the house actually *looked* much different, just that it felt different. The only time I nearly cried was when I went into the utility room. There was an empty peg where Tony's jacket usually hangs. Mum was probably feeling relieved that he'd gone because now the horrible atmosphere had gone too. And yet when I passed her on the landing I could see tears in her eyes, and her chin all wobbly.

But why? This is what Mum wants, isn't it?

On Monday night Tony phoned. We talked about what I'd been doing at school, which took about twenty seconds, then his voice suddenly switched into bright and cheerful mode.

'Listen, Han, I've done something that you and Rachel are going to be very pleased about! I've booked the big hall at the leisure centre for a week on Saturday at six-thirty. Let's keep it a secret from Rachel, shall we? So you invite her friends – you know better than me who to invite, no more than twenty – and I'll sort everything else. All right?'

I knew I should have been delighted about the disco, but I was worried because everything was different from usual, and I could tell it meant trouble. Since Tony had been in our family, if Rachel had a party or a treat, it was always organised by Tigs and Simon, and though *I* would be invited, it had nothing to do with Tony. Then if Tony wanted to organise his own thing with Mum, he could. But never *ever* did Tony organise anything with Tigs because Mum would have gone mad. Of course it was obvious there was no way Tony would ever dream of organising this disco with Mum, now things were so bad between them. But I couldn't imagine Tony doing something on his own. So that only left one answer . . .

'What did Mum say about it?' I asked carefully.

Tony sounded suddenly firm. 'It's nothing to do with Mum now, Han.'

'You mean . . . she's not going to be there?'

'I don't think she'd want to be there.'

There was a silence while I got the courage together to ask the big question.

'Will Tigs be there?' I held my breath.

'Yes, of course. She helped me arrange it all.'

So I guessed right. How could Tony do this to poor Mum? But I didn't want to say anything in case I made things worse.

'So what do you reckon?' Tony carried on cheerfully. 'Do we tell Rach or keep it a secret?'

I couldn't help sounding flat. 'I think it's better if she knows, so she can invite who she wants.'

'OK then, love. If you think that's best . . . And I'll give you a ring again tomorrow – or you ring me if you want. Any time. You've got my work number, haven't you?'

'Craig?'

No answer. He'd got his music turned right up.

I was standing outside his bedroom door, planning what to say to him that wouldn't make him flip. He got angry so easily these days. All I wanted to do was talk to him about Rachel's party. I knew Mum would be in a real state if she found out that Tony and Tigs had arranged a party together. She'd think they were deliberately trying to spite her. I began to consider not even telling Mum and just hoping like mad she never found out. I'd have to fix it so I stayed over at Rachel's that night, and I'd pack my disco clothes without her knowing. As long as I could get Tony to keep quiet about it, everything would be fine.

Craig wasn't answering my knock. He probably didn't hear it with all the noise.

'Can I come in?' I called through the door.

I wasn't sure if he'd heard me, or if he'd answered, so I just waited, and after a few seconds he turned the music down, which I took to be my cue to go in. He was sitting at his desk and didn't turn round.

'Tony's hired the hall at the leisure centre for Rachel's party,' I launched straight in.

No answer.

'Mum doesn't know . . .'

'So?'

'Do you think she might find out?'

'Probably.'

'Do you think she'd be sad if she did?'

'Probably.'

What a dead-end conversation this was turning out to be. I decided to bring up the thing that was worrying me the most. It felt like I was dragging the words out of the very centre of my body but I was desperately hoping Craig might tell me I'd got it all wrong, and Mum wasn't going anywhere.

'When we went to Granny's at the weekend I overheard Granny say something about Mum getting right away from Tony...'

'Yeah?'

Why did he sound so unbothered?

'She's not, is she?'

'Well, if she thinks *I'm* going with her, she's got another think coming.'

'Has she said anything to you?'

'No. But I guess they'll sell the house and split the proceeds.'

'And... what about me?'

'Then you'll have a bit of a decision to make, won't you?'

My insides felt as though they were being dissolved by a powerful chemical or something.

'Wh-what decision?'

''Bye-'bye Rachel or 'bye-'bye Mum?'

I felt like laying into Craig with my fists. How could he sit there with his back to me, saying these horrible things about making decisions? He never used to be like this.

'I don't want to leave Rachel,' I managed to utter.

'So live with Tony then. It's your choice.'

'But I'd miss Mum too much. And I don't want to choose!'

And with that I burst into tears and ran out of the room.

Part of me wanted to rush up to Mum and confront her with what Craig had said to me, and shout and shout and sob and scream until she changed her mind. But the rest of me still thought that if I didn't mention the name Granny, the whole idea of her moving might be forgotten.

The next day I was desperate to talk to Rachel, but I hardly saw her at school during the day because she had to work on a group project with her friends at break times and lunchtime.

Instead of catching the bus we walked home from school, even though it was quite a long way, because I wanted plenty of time to break the awful news.

Rachel listened wide-eyed, gasping a few times as I talked. When I'd finished there was a silence, as though she was too stunned to speak. Eventually she said in a very soft voice, 'But you're not absolutely certain she's moving, are you?'

'No, but Craig didn't sound at all surprised when I told him. Only I daren't talk to Mum about it. It's like, if I talk about it, it's sure to happen, but the longer nobody mentions it, the more chance there is that she might change her mind or something.'

'Will you definitely have to live with your mum?'

'Craig says I can live with Tony if I say that that's what I want.'

'So . . . will you say that?'

'I don't know what to say. I couldn't bear to be so far from Mum.'

Something hardened in Rachel's voice. 'But you don't mind being so far from me?'

I couldn't believe it. She was suggesting that I could leave Mum – just like that.

'But . . . she's my mum . . .'

And then I got a shock because Rachel suddenly lost her temper. 'She shouldn't move away then, should she? It's cruel. She's not thinking about your feelings at all. Why can't she just stay where she is?'

This wasn't how the conversation was supposed to go. I'd thought we'd both comfort each other like mad, then start planning what we could do to try and get Mum to change her mind. But here we were arguing. Maybe I hadn't explained very well.

'I asked Craig what would happen with the house and he said he thought they'd sell it and split the money from the sale,' I tried to explain as calmly as possible. 'You see, at the moment it's not fair on Tony because he has to keep paying half the mortgage as well as the rent on his flat.'

Rachel's voice rose even more. 'Why can't your mum pay all the mortgage as she's the one living in the house?'

'She can't afford it. She only works part time.'

'She should have thought of that before she kicked my dad out.'

'She didn't kick him out. They arranged it together.'

What was happening? This was turning into a terrible row. But Rachel and I never rowed.

'So how come Dad isn't staying in the house? Your mum ought to be the one to move into a little poky flat. She'd be able to afford that.'

I could feel myself getting angrier. Rachel was being so horrible to Mum.

'Because Mum's the one with us two. There

wouldn't be room for three people in a little flat,' I said, raising my voice to match hers.

'Well, you and Craig can stay in the house with Dad then.'

'Tony wouldn't be able to do all the shopping and cooking and cleaning and everything as well as a full-time job, would he? Mum has to do all that – and she does her job as well, *and* buys us clothes and takes us everywhere in the car . . . That's why they were always arguing because Tony doesn't help with anything and if anything needs doing that Mum can't do, he always leaves it for weeks and weeks and tells her that she's nagging if she dares to mention it.'

'Wasn't very smart of her getting rid of him, then, was it? Now she's got to do even more herself. And anyway I've heard your mum nagging, and I'm not surprised my dad got hacked off with it. I bet if she shut up, Dad'd do everything.'

'I've told you, she didn't get rid of him!' I shouted.

This was unbelievable. Rachel was talking as though she knew more about my family than I did. Fancy saying that Craig and I should live with Tony while Mum went off into a little flat.

'Anyway, it would be pretty stupid us living with Tony instead of Mum. He's not even our real dad.'

The moment the words were out of my mouth I wished I could shovel them back in again.

Suddenly Rachel was yelling. 'D'you think I don't know that? He's *mine*. And I wish he'd never left Mum to go and live with *your* mum in the first place.'

Her voice cracked at the end of the sentence. The last two words were more like crying than talking. But still I couldn't help defending Mum.

'Maybe it was the other way round and *your*

mum got fed up with him, same as *my* mum has.'

And that was when Rachel ran off. And I was left there. Alone. The cars were still passing, the sun was still shining, everything was exactly as it had been a minute before, and yet to me it felt as though the world had ended.

5 THE BOND

'Your mum doesn't seem screwed up or anything,' said my friend Katie.

'Yeah, she just seems to be carrying on same as normal,' said Naomi.

Katie and Naomi had come home from school with me, because we were working on an English project in groups of three. I really wanted to go to one of their houses, but they both wanted to come to mine. I think they secretly fancy Craig. God knows why. I bet they soon change their minds once they see him being all bolshie and hard.

They were right about Mum seeming happy though. I know I was only young when my real dad left us, but I can remember Mum getting gradually happier after he'd gone. And now it seemed as though the same thing was happening again. In a way I didn't want her to be happy. If she was still miserable then maybe she'd realise how awful it was without Tony and she'd try and sort things out with him so he could come back. I knew I was being pathetic but I couldn't help building castles in the air, imagining how magic and brilliant it would be if they suddenly realised they'd made a big mistake, and decided to get back together again.

The thing that was eating away at me all the time, was that Rachel and I hadn't spoken to each other for a whole day. I didn't look at her in assembly and I avoided her at break time and lunchtime. I'd passed her twice in the corridor when we'd each been with friends from our own year. The first time she'd looked down and the second time we'd both pretended to be deep in conversations with our friends.

It was unbearable being bad friends with Rachel. We haven't had a single argument since the day we first met. It was just before Tony left her mum. Rachel and I were both at primary and I had to take a message to the staff room from one of the teachers, during lesson time. When I got there I found this girl who was younger than me standing by the door with her fist in the air ready to knock. When she saw me, she burst into tears and said she couldn't knock because she'd got a message but she'd forgotten what to say. I felt really sorry for her and tried to help her remember. Then one of the teachers came out and saw Rachel in tears and me comforting her. She took us into the staff room, and talked sympathetically to us about how it would all be all right in the end. Neither Rachel nor I had a clue what she was on about. It was quite a long time later that I realised that the teachers must have known about Mum and Tony before Rachel and I did.

After that Rachel started looking for me at play times. It was as though that teacher had helped to bond us. Because that's how we've been ever since. Bonded. Until now.

Whenever I think back to our terrible row I feel angrier than ever with Mum and Tony. They're messing up my life, and I don't know why I'm being nice to either of them. They don't deserve it. I wonder if Rachel is still angry with me or whether she's feeling sad now, like I am.

When Katie, Naomi and I had finished working on our project we went down to watch telly. We were deep into this new American soap when Craig came in. He was smoking. I couldn't believe it. Mum and Tony are dead against smoking.

'Craig! Has Mum seen you smoking?'

'Uh-huh.'

'Didn't she say anything?'

'Nah. 'Cos she knows there's nothing she can do about it.'

He sat down with a saucer on the arm of the chair and tapped at his cigarette every so often like someone who'd been smoking for years. I saw Katie and Naomi glance at him a few times, and wondered if they still thought he was cool. Probably not. It was so embarrassing. And feeling embarrassed made me feel cross. Everything was falling apart. Mum should be telling Craig not to smoke. And he should be obeying her.

At the end of the programme Katie's mum arrived to take Katie and Naomi home. I bet they all talked in the car about Craig and me and Mum. I knew Katie and Naomi would try and defend me and my family, but I also knew it wouldn't really work, and that made me feel helpless.

Smoked three cigarettes? Whatever is Hannah's mother thinking about?

*Hannah's mum and stepdad have jut split up,
Mum.*

Oh well, that explains it then. Poor Craig . . .

'It's lovely to see your friends round here,' said
Mum, once they'd gone. I didn't comment.
'Er . . . you haven't borrowed any money from
my purse have you? Only I seem to be ten
pounds short . . .'

'I haven't borrowed anything,' I said. 'Maybe
Craig did –' I couldn't resist seeing what she'd
say to this next bit – 'to pay for his cigarettes.'

She shot me a quick glance. I'd hit a nerve.
'Craig's going through a difficult time at the
moment. I don't approve of him smoking, of
course, but I'm letting it go for the moment.'

I felt angry. 'Don't you think *I* might be
going through a difficult time too?'

'Yes, I know it's just as bad for you, love. And
I'm really proud of the way you're handling it so
well.'

Huh!

I started shouting, because I'd totally lost my temper. 'So just because I'm not smoking, you think I'm handling it well. Well, I'm not! And it's all your fault. You can't even stop Craig from smoking. If Tony was here he'd be able to.'

And then Mum shouted too. 'But he's not here, is he? I can't help that, can I?'

'Yes, you can. You shouldn't have let him go in the first place!' I wanted to punish her even more for making me feel this way. 'I'm going out.'

'You can't just go. Where are you going?'

'To Rachel's.'

I didn't turn round – just walked out. Mum was probably in tears, and even though I'd just been so angry with her, it twisted me up inside to imagine her sitting with her elbows on the table and her head in her hands, her fingers rubbing hard into her cheeks and forehead, like she did these days.

My head was so full of thoughts that I didn't notice my journey to Rachel's at all. In fact, if a time machine had landed right in front of me I don't think I would have been aware of it.

When I was almost there, I came back to earth and stopped in my tracks.

What are you going to do now, Hannah? Go in and say hi and act as though nothing's gone wrong between you?

I scanned all the windows to see if anyone was watching me. It didn't look like it. Then I spotted something that made my heart thump against my ribs. Tony's car was parked outside. This was the very thing I most dreaded happening. But I never really thought it *would* happen. After all this time, it was as though Tony was breaking the rules that the adults had made for themselves — *Tony and Mum, Simon and Tigs, and never shall the two pairs have anything to do with each other.*

Maybe Tony absolutely *had* to pop in to give

something to Rachel . . . I couldn't imagine what, I was just trying to make excuses for why he was here. If Mum knew, she'd be so upset.

I stood there trying to decide whether to turn round and go straight home or whether to stay and see if I could make everything right again between me and Rachel. It would be easier just to go home, but I was so curious about what Tony was doing here. If he'd made friends with Tigs and Simon it would be great for Rachel but terrible for me, because that would make an even bigger rift between Mum and him.

As I stood there dithering I had another picture of little Rachel crying outside the staff room door. And it was that made me rush up to the front door.

I knocked quickly before I lost my courage. Then the moment I'd knocked I wished I could run away, like a naughty kid playing a prank, because I was scared in case Rachel might have told them I was taking Mum's side, and they didn't like me any more.

But it was too late. Someone was coming to answer the door.

6 HAPPY FAMILIES

'Hello, Hannah,' said Simon, opening the door with a welcoming smile on his face. 'Look who it is, everyone,' he said as he put a hand on my back to steer me into the kitchen.

Walking into that room I understood the saying *Time stood still . . .*

Sitting round the table, grinning at Rachel's sister, Susannah, sat Tony, Tigs and Rachel, their empty plates and half-full glasses in front of them. Susannah was centre stage, by the window, with a funny expression on her face. It looked as though she was in the middle of imitating someone – like a teacher – and the others were enjoying her performance. And now I'd come along and interrupted their fun.

Rachel met my eyes for a split second. I couldn't fail to see the shock in them before she looked back at Susannah. It was impossible to tell if she was still cross or if she felt embarrassed about me turning up like that, especially seeing Tony there. He looked very uncomfortable. Good. I hated seeing him with this family. It was so unfair on Mum. I should never have come. I felt like I did one time in the school playground when I was much younger and suddenly found myself surrounded by people from another gang, who were trying to get me to swap gangs and join theirs.

It was Tigs who took charge. 'Hello, Hannah,' she said, jumping up and grabbing a chair from the far corner of the room. 'Move up, everyone – make room for Hannah.'

And it was only then that time stopped standing still.

'Hello, love,' said Tony, trying to sound casual. (He failed.) 'This is a . . . nice surprise.'

His words left a big question mark hanging in the air. I bet he was wondering why I'd turned up without warning, whether Mum and I had had a row, whether Mum even knew that I was here, whether something terrible had happened. I wasn't sure if Rachel would have told him that she and I had had a massive argument. But I just sat down, and tried to look as though everything was fine and I wasn't at all embarrassed about being here with Tony and there was absolutely nothing wrong between Rachel and me.

I was praying that she might suggest we went up to her room. If she'd only do that one little thing, I wouldn't mind being the one to apologise even though I didn't really think I was to blame. But she just sat there ignoring me, and I could see that Tigs was puzzled, though no one else seemed to have noticed anything wrong.

'We've been planning the birthday party of the year,' said Tony, rubbing his hands and grinning all over his face. 'It's going to be a goody,' he added excitedly. 'Tell Hannah who your mum's managed to book, Rach.'

I looked at Rachel, but she didn't look back – just answered in a flat sort of voice. 'Pete Jawaski . . . We're having a disco.'

I didn't even know if I was invited, but I had to say something, because this was more than just a local DJ.

'Cool!'

Then everybody started chipping in about what fun it was going to be, what music might be played, what the lighting would be like. Simon even suggested having a dance competition and a prize for the winner. I tried to smile and look like I was sharing everyone's excitement, but inside I felt all churned up.

Susannah was gripping the back of my chair and rocking backwards and forwards on it.

'Rachel's going to have three parents at her party this year!' she told me excitedly. 'She's never had all three before!'

There was a silence, then Simon coughed, and Tigs started offering people drinks as though they were going out of fashion. Susannah blushed. She must have suddenly clicked that she'd said something a bit hurtful to me. It was as though everyone had shone a big bright torch on my loneliness, so now it was perfectly clear that I was the poor little girl with no happy family at home, while lucky Rachel had got a happy family of her own plus an extra bit of mine.

'I only came to say hello,' I said quickly, when Tigs started pouring lemonade in a glass for me. 'I'd better go now.'

* * *

I could tell Mum had been crying. Her eyes looked red-rimmed even though she'd tried to cover it up with more make-up than usual. She jumped up when I went in through the back door.

'Are you all right, Han?'

A few minutes ago I'd felt so sorry for her that all I'd wanted to do was give her a great big hug, but now I was actually here, I felt cross with her again.

'Where's Craig?' I asked.

'Watching television in the other room. Would you like a cup of tea?'

She was trying to be nice and friendly. It just made me want to be even more horrible to her.

'No . . .' It's funny but although I was in a bad mood I still thought I'd better say 'thank you', so I did. Then I went out of the kitchen, because if Mum thought she'd got round me, she had another think coming.

Craig was sitting there coughing away in front

of the telly. There were six cigarette stubs on the saucer. I wanted to talk to him – or was it more that I wanted *him* to talk to me? But I didn't know what to say, because he hadn't even said hi when I'd gone in the room.

'I've just been round to Rachel's.'

'Good for you.'

I tried to ignore that.

'Tony was there.'

I'd got him interested. His face had stopped looking as though it was made of stone.

'What was *he* doing there?'

It sounded like Craig hated Tony the way he almost spat out the word *he*.

'That party for Rachel I told you about – well, he's organised it with Tigs. I mean, she's going to be there too. And Simon. Everyone except Mum, in fact.'

Craig swore. At least I think he did – it was under his breath. His eyes went into staring mode then fastened back on the telly. It looked like our conversation had come to an end. But I wanted it to go on. I wanted to talk more about Rachel's party, and I wanted him to say things that I knew there was no hope of him saying – that he was only smoking to get at Mum, that he'd stop as soon as he finished this packet. Things like that.

I suddenly remembered about Mum's missing ten pounds. It had to be Craig. I tried to sound as though I was in on a secret with him. 'Did you buy that packet of cigarettes out of your allowance, Craig?'

'Josh Rogers gave them me.'

Josh Rogers . . . That reminded me . . .

'Josh was looking for you the other day at school.'

'He'd have a job finding me. I don't go to school.'

DON'T, not DIDN'T.

'What?' I could only manage a thin trailing whisper.

'You heard.'

'But you *do* go to school. You have to. You've got GCSEs and it's the law.'

I knew I must sound about six and a half.

'I don't have to do *any*thing.'

'Does Mum know?'

'Nah.' There was a silence. I was still standing by the door. I felt as though someone had frozen me and left me right there, staring at a bit of fluff on the carpet. I knew Craig was looking at me though. 'You dare tell her . . .' my frozen statue self didn't speak . . . 'and I'll have to tell her about Rachel's party, won't I?'

7 SORTED

Mum came into the living-room and sat down on the settee. She was trying to look casual, as though she was just watching telly. I wanted to see if she was going to say anything to Craig about smoking, so I went and sat on the settee beside her. Not too close. Not too friendly.

'I was thinking about Rachel's party,' Mum began, turning to me with a bright smile. My heart started drumming. 'I thought I might contact Tony and suggest hiring a hall somewhere.'

Omigod! She's trying to make up for all the

horrible stuff that's been going on. This is your cue, Hannah. Just tell her that Tony's already hired a hall.

But I couldn't make myself speak. Surely she must have been able to hear my heart beating. She was right next to me and it sounded like a big bass drum to me. Craig's eyes flickered as he calmly took out another cigarette and lit it. He coughed when he drew the smoke in, but then he kept his mouth closed, probably to stop the cough being so obvious. The smoke just made him choke though, and for the first time for a long time I noticed Mum's eyes twinkle, as though she was having a private joke with herself. At first I thought it was a bit cruel of her to be secretly smiling when her son was having a coughing fit, but then I suddenly saw the funny side of it too, and I couldn't help a little snigger escaping. Unfortunately, Craig heard.

He sat bolt upright and fixed me with an accusing stare. Then he tried to speak, but it just made him break into another spasm of coughing. What happened next really surprised me. Mum got up, took the cigarette out of his hand and stubbed it out hard in the saucer. Then she moved the saucer on to the little corner table.

'Oi! What yer doing? I was smoking that!' Craig managed to splutter.

Mum didn't bat an eyelid. 'Yes, I was aware of that, Craig.'

Craig stood up as though to get the saucer back, but Mum spoke very sharply. 'Sit down.'

I held my breath. Craig might be about to really flip now. I was dreading it in case he blurted out that Tony and Tigs had already hired a hall for Rachel's party. But incredibly he sat down. It was odd, but I felt pleased that Mum had been so firm. It was kind of a relief to know that someone was in charge in this house, otherwise goodness knows what Craig would do next.

'As I was saying,' said Mum, 'I'm going to suggest to Tony that we hire the leisure centre hall for Rachel's party.' She smiled at me, then Craig, then me again. 'What do you think? Good idea, eh?' I gulped and tried to smile. 'I thought you'd be jumping for joy, Han. What's the matter?'

'N-nothing. It's a great idea . . . only what if it's already booked? I know the leisure centre is really popular. Katie said that her mum tried to hire the big hall there and even though she gave them a whole month's notice, it was booked already . . .'

Craig was staring sullenly at the telly with his arms folded and his shoulders hunched. Mum carried on enthusiastically.

'We'll have to get on to it quickly then. But it doesn't matter if it's a couple of weeks later than her actual birthday, does it? It'll give her something to look forward to. I've just been trying to get hold of Tony, but there's no reply. I'll try again later.'

I pretended I was going to check my e-mail, but instead I got the phone from the hall and took it up to my room. There, I tapped in Rachel's number.

It was Rachel who answered, which threw me, because I'd been prepared for Tigs or Simon.

'Hi . . . it's me. Can I speak to Tony please.'

She sounded pretty taken aback too. 'Hold on a sec.'

Tony took ages to get to the phone. I was worried that Mum might come up and catch me.

'Hi, Han. All right?'

I launched straight in. 'The trouble is, Mum's going to phone you about a party for Rachel. She suddenly thought about hiring the leisure centre. I didn't dare tell her that you'd already done it because I thought she might be upset – you know, because of Tigs and everything.'

There was a pause while Tony worked out what I was talking about. When he spoke he didn't sound at all fazed.

'Nah, you don't want to worry about that, Han. When your mum phones me I'll just tell her she doesn't have to worry about it because it's sorted, OK?'

I could imagine Tony saying that on the phone to Mum. Mum would want to know what he meant by sorted, then he'd tell her that he and Tigs had organised it and then Mum would feel totally gutted, because she'd suddenly realise that Tony was friendly with Tigs again, and that would hurt her even more. And even if Tony invited her she wouldn't want to go. She'd feel like an outsider.

'The thing is, I don't think Mum would want to go,' I said carefully.

'No problem. I hadn't imagined she would.'

'Well, could you pretend it's just Tigs and Simon doing it?'

'I don't think your mum'll care two hoots that I'm going to be there too,' said Tony, laughing lightly. 'I am Rachel's dad, after all.'

I wasn't sure what to say next. I just wanted him to understand how left out Mum would feel if we were all at the party except her. The trouble was I wasn't even sure that *I* was invited. Maybe Tony would give me a clue.

'I know – but it's because you'll be there with Tigs and Simon, and if . . . I'm there too, Mum might feel a bit left out.'

'Don't you worry yourself about it, love. It'll be fine, you'll see.'

I wasn't getting through to Tony, and I was beginning to feel desperate. This was just the kind of thing that would make Mum want to move near Granny more than ever.

The click of the living-room door opening made me speed up.

'OK. Can you tell Rachel I'll see her tomorrow in morning break behind the food technology block?'

'Tomorrow morning break behind the food

technology block. Sounds a bit dodgy! What are you two up to?'

I could hear the laughter in his voice.

'Nothing. You won't forget to tell her, will you.'

'I shall pass the message on right away, love. And I'll give you and Craig a ring tomorrow evening.'

I rang off in the nick of time. There were footsteps right at the top of the stairs and it didn't sound like Craig's heavy clodhoppers.

'Can I come in?' said Mum.

She sat down on my bed.

'You didn't seem all that happy about my idea,' she began.

'No, I think it's good, only . . . I think Simon and Tigs have got something organised now.'

'Oh right . . . Well, Tony might want to do something else. I'll try him again soon.'

She studied the posters on my wall before she went out. I knew very well that she wasn't at all interested in my pop idols. She was giving me time in case I wanted to talk to her about Tony or separations or Craig. Well, I didn't want to discuss those horrible topics. Not with her and not with anyone. Except Rachel.

It was ten-twenty and I was in geography. I couldn't take in a single word Mr Harrison was saying because I was so tense about meeting Rachel. When I'd been talking to Tony on the phone it had seemed easy to ask him to give Rachel a message. But now I was scared stiff. What if Rachel didn't bother to come? What if she sent one of her friends to tell me to stop pestering her? What if she came, but told me that she didn't want to be my friend any more?

Before assembly, Katie and Naomi had been quizzing me on what had gone wrong between Rachel and me. I'd tried to explain about it all being to do with Mum and Tony splitting up, but I'd got the feeling that they thought the argument was partly my fault. They didn't actually say it – I could just tell.

The moment the bell went I made my way to the food technology block. I looked at my watch about every ten seconds but ten to eleven came and went, then five to, then eleven o'clock.

I started making excuses for her. The teacher kept them in at the end of the last lesson . . . she had extra choir practice . . . extra gym practice . . . Tony forgot to tell her . . .

Who was I trying to kid? Rachel didn't want to see me. She thought I was siding with Mum against her dad, and she didn't like it. Maybe I *was* – a bit. But only a bit. All I wanted was to be friends again. But now Rachel had refused to even meet me and talk about it, I felt hurt. Very hurt and very angry.

The bell for the end of break rang and I walked off across the netball courts to French. My school bag suddenly felt as though it weighed a tonne.

8 THE KITCHEN – BEFORE
AND AFTER

'You were right about Rachel's party,' said Mum, practically the moment I walked in through the back door at the end of school. 'I eventually got hold of Tony last night and he said Rachel had told him Simon and Tigs were organising something for her, after all.'

I breathed a huge sigh of relief. At least I didn't have to worry about that now. Tony must have decided to keep quiet about what was really happening with Rachel and the party. I wouldn't be going to the party anyway, now that Rachel had made it clear she didn't want to make up. So I might as well just forget it.

'Oh no!' Mum suddenly said.

'What?'

'I think the man with the logs is here.'

She belted outside to move her car out on to the road so the pick-up van could drop the logs in the drive. We get a delivery about once every three months for the woodburner, and it takes all four of us to stack it up at the side of the house. My heart sank at the thought of doing it all without Tony. And the way Craig was at the moment, we weren't likely to get any help from him either. Which left me and Mum. Great.

'We'll have to do it a bit at a time, that's all there is for it,' said Mum in a tired voice when she came back in. 'There's nothing I can do today though, because I've booked a hairdresser's appointment.' I couldn't help showing my surprise. Mum's never been all that keen on going to the hairdresser's. 'I looked at myself in the mirror this morning and I thought, *Caroline, you look a mess.* So I decided to do something about it.'

'You look fine,' I said. But I knew I didn't sound convincing.

After Mum had gone I switched the kettle on. It sounded so loud. Even the clock ticking sounded loud. I looked round the kitchen and I saw it as a *room* for the first time ever. Usually I didn't see it all. It was a sort of background to our family. But now I noticed how the paintwork was dirty on the wall near the sink and there were two big cobwebs in one corner of the ceiling. The area round the sink was very tidy and gleaming. The mat in front of the woodburner was worn out. The table top was faded. The dresser looked bright and beautiful – painted mottled blue. The flowers on the windowsill were wilting. I gave them more water and talked to them as I was doing it, but my voice sounded stupid on its own in this kitchen

– like my body wasn't there, only my voice.

I've hardly ever been on my own in the house before. It doesn't worry me, being alone here. I'm thirteen and it's daytime, and Craig'll probably be home soon, but right now the house doesn't feel like a home. It feels like an empty building – like we've *all* moved out. Not just Tony. Maybe I'm psychic and I'm having a premonition.

As I stood there in the middle of the kitchen I heard footsteps coming up to the back door. *Good. Craig's back already. Maybe the house will go back to feeling like a home now.* A few seconds later the kitchen door opened and in came Tony.

His face lit up when he saw me. 'Hiya, Han. I wondered if you were out with your mum when I saw her car wasn't there.'

'She's gone to the hairdresser's – and Craig's out. Don't know where.'

'All on your own then?' He went over to the kettle and switched it back on. I couldn't help staring. It was funny how he acted like he lived here even though he didn't. 'Let's have a nice cup of tea.'

'Did Mum know you were coming? Is that why she's gone out?'

'She told me she was going to the hairdresser's and I said I might pop round so you wouldn't be on your own.'

'Mum never mentioned that.'

'I told her not to, because I couldn't guarantee I'd be able to get off work early, and I didn't want you to be hanging around expecting me.'

'I've got biology homework. Do you know anything about genes?'

'Only the blue denim sort.'

'I'll have to wait for Craig then, because I don't get it at all.'

'OK, and while we're waiting let's go and stack some of those logs, eh?'

My eyes must have been goggling I was so gobsmacked. If Tony had still been living with us I'm sure he'd never have been so keen to get stacking logs. It was always Mum who rounded us all up and made us get on with it. If it had been left up to Tony we would have waited months.

'What about the tea?' was all I could manage to utter.

'Changed my mind. We'll have it later when we've earned it.'

He rubbed his hands and headed out of the front door as though he was a boxer getting ready to defend his title.

An hour later we'd done the lot. I'm sure it used to take an hour when all four of us did it, and yet Tony and I had managed on our own in the same time. It was so satisfying sitting in the warm kitchen afterwards, drinking tea and listening to one of Craig's CDs. It turned out that Tony knew quite a bit about genes because half an hour later my biology homework was done too.

'What are you lot eating tonight?' he asked.

I shrugged. 'Mum didn't say.'

'Why don't you get something ready for when she gets back?'

My eyes went back to goggling mode. 'Are you . . . staying to eat with us?' I asked tentatively, feeling a little surge of happiness zoom up from my stomach.

'No, no . . .' He looked at his watch, and I guessed he was working out that Mum would be back any minute. 'I've got to make a move now, Han. But I'll see you at the weekend, eh?'

I wanted to talk to him about Rachel and me and the party – explain that I wouldn't be there. But when I opened my mouth to speak I couldn't find the right words. So I just said, 'Yeah, OK.'

And he grinned and went.

After Tony had gone I looked round the kitchen and saw it in a completely different way. It was back to being the kitchen again. Even the flowers seemed to have stopped wilting. I decided to start the meal to help Mum. I defrosted some chicken pieces, then chopped them up and began to fry them in the wok. When all the pieces had cooked I added some korma sauce – we often have chicken korma – and settled down to my maths.

About ten minutes later Mum came back.

'Hey! It looks really nice!' I told her. 'Have you had it coloured?'

'Just a few highlights. But never mind my hair – I think you and Craig deserve medals!'

I didn't know what she was on about at first, then I realised. 'Oh no, it was me and Tony. Craig isn't back yet.'

Mum stopped in her tracks on her way to

hang her coat up in the utility room. 'Tony? Tony came?' I nodded, smiling. Her mouth was practically hanging open. 'And you and he did all those logs together?' I nodded again. 'I bet he took a fair bit of persuading, didn't he?'

'It was his idea actually.'

Mum shook her head as though wonders would never cease. Then she saw the chicken cooking in the wok and gave me a big smile.

'What a lovely surprise to come home to!'

'I was just about to put the rice in, but I didn't know how long you'd be.'

'You carry on with your homework, Han. I'll do the rice.'

Craig came back just as we'd finished eating. He stank of cigarettes. He took off his coat and put it on the back of one of the chairs, sat down and started helping himself to rice.

'Where have you been?' said Mum, standing

up with her hands on her hips and fixing Craig with a cross look.

'Oh, spare me the dramatics, Mum,' he sneered as he kept serving himself. 'I don't have to tell you anything and there's no point in getting heavy because it doesn't work. I've seen through the sham. Kids don't *have* to obey their parents – especially not when they're pushing sixteen.'

He'd taken every last bit of the rice and the korma. He leaned forwards and started tucking into his meal as though it was his first for days.

'That's very true,' said Mum. Her voice was completely steady, but I could see the anger in her eyes. 'Kids don't have to obey their parents, and come to think of it, I don't think there's anything written into my contract that says I have to provide food for you, is there?'

She leaned over, grabbed his plate walked over to the bin and scraped the meal into it. Then she put the plate in the dishwasher and started clearing our two plates. My heart was pounding, but I was glad that she'd got one over on Craig. I hated it when he threw his weight around.

Craig himself was sitting there looking totally gobsmacked. Then he slowly got up, walked over to Mum's handbag, helped himself to a ten pound note from her purse and made for the door.

'I'll just have to go to the chippy then.'

Mum was shaking. I looked from her to Craig, and I couldn't bear this horrible new brother. I stood up and it was as though I'd pressed a button and released my anger. It surged up from my toes and gathered strength as it rushed through my body. When I spoke my voice must have been heavy with it, because Craig stopped and listened for once.

'Yeah, get lost, Craig! And on your way out look at the logs. I could have done with you earlier on – but you couldn't care less about anyone but your selfish self, could you? Thanks for being such a good, strong, reliable big brother. It's so helpful that you walk away at the first sign of trouble.'

I stopped, exhausted, and held my breath. Mum seemed to be doing the same. Craig stood there for what seemed like ages. I knew he'd be torn – wondering whether to lose face and come back, or go anyway, which would be like admitting that he was selfish and weak.

Finally he pulled the door closed behind him and walked off. Selfishness won. I flopped back into my chair, suddenly drained.

Mum came and put her arm round me, her cheek against mine.

'It doesn't matter that he's gone. You've broken through that heavy armour he's been wearing lately. It was brilliant what you said.' I heard the tremor in her voice. 'Brilliant!'

9 SUSSING CRAIG

The following Monday Naomi, Katie and I were talking about Craig at lunchtime in the canteen.

'I think you ought to tell your mum, Han,' said Naomi. 'Craig might be getting into big trouble. You don't know where he goes when he's not at school, do you?'

'That's a point,' said Katie, frowning. 'Where *does* he go? I mean, he's been bunking off for days now!'

She was right. I thought he'd pack it in now it was a new week, but he'd bunked off again today.

'I've no idea where he goes. He leaves the house about ten minutes before I do wearing his uniform and carrying his school bag.'

'So why don't you follow him one day?'

'But then *I'd* be skiving too.'

Naomi suddenly beckoned with her hand for us to lean forwards, so we went into a huddle at our end of the dinner table.

'Let's all three follow him. It wouldn't matter missing school just for one day – one morning, in fact.'

'The teachers are going to get a bit suspicious if we're all absent on the same morning. What excuse do we give?'

'One of us can have the dentist, one can be ill, and one can miss the bus. Simple.'

Katie and I laughed. It was the way Naomi had got it all worked out, and she came out with this whole string of really glib excuses.

'The dentist?' said Katie wrinkling her nose. 'That's pretty boring.'

My imagination started doing overtime. 'Yeah, I think I'll invent a St Bernard's dog that's really ill and has to go the vet. It's too heavy for one person to carry, so Mum needs me to help get it in and out of the car. Yeah, that would take a whole morning, wouldn't it?'

Katie and Naomi laughed, and Chris Carter and Sean Jenkins, who were sitting just along from them, wanted to know what was so funny. We told them we were inventing ridiculous reasons for being off school and they joined in.

Then Chris suddenly turned serious. 'What excuse does your brother make for bunking off?' he asked me.

'I – I'm not sure,' I stammered.

'Don't your mum and dad know?' Chris went on.

I shook my head.

'You ought to tell them. He might start shoplifting, then do bigger robberies. He could even end up in prison, you know!'

'Thanks for that, Chris!' said Katie sarcastically, but jokingly.

'I agree with Chris,' said Naomi.

I knew then that I was going to have to do something about it. Another big worry that wouldn't go away on its own.

When I was clearing my plates away at the counter, I suddenly found I was standing right next to Rachel. Our eyes met for a second, then we both looked away.

'I don't get you two,' whispered Katie as we walked out of the canteen. 'How can best friends stop being best friends just because of one argument? Don't you think it's time you made up?'

I'd never told Katie and Naomi about waiting behind the food technology block for a whole break, but I decided to now.

'I tried to make up, but Rachel obviously didn't want to.'

'What? You said sorry and everything?'

'No, I left a message with Tony to tell her to meet me the next day behind the food technology block, and she never came. I waited for the whole of break.' I couldn't help going a bit pink because at the time I'd told Katie and Naomi that one of the teachers had collared me to help her carry some supplies to the food technology block. Neither of them mentioned that now, thank goodness.

'Maybe Tony forgot to tell her.'

'No, he definitely would have told her because he was at her house when I rang him. *And* I reminded him at the end of the phone call, when I knew he'd be seeing her straight away.'

Naomi gave me a sympathetic smile, but didn't say anything. I suppose there was nothing more to be said.

In library period that afternoon, Katie, Naomi and I managed to get a table which was out of view of the teacher. You're not supposed to talk in the library, but if you get the corner table you can at least whisper.

'Are you going to follow Craig tomorrow?' Naomi asked.

'I'd better not miss maths.'

'The next day then.'

'I'm not sure if I dare. I mean, what will I do when I see where he's gone?'

'Nothing. But at least you'll know then.'

'What good will that be?'

Naomi frowned. I could see her brain ticking over, trying to find an answer to that one. 'Because . . .' she whispered slowly, playing for time, 'then you could tell your mum . . . and she could pretend that she saw him herself. That'd get you off the hook, but get Craig found out.' She smiled triumphantly at Katie and me.

I still wasn't sure. 'What if Craig saw me?'

'You have to make sure he doesn't.' Naomi raised her voice in her excitement. 'Go on! Let's all go.'

'You'll all be going to the head in a minute if you don't stop talking!' said Mrs James, the most horrible teacher in the school. She must have crept up on us, so she could catch us out.

When she'd gone, Katie did a mime to show that she'd got her piano lesson that morning, so she wouldn't be able to come. Naomi then wrote on a bit of paper, *You and me, Han. OK?*

I wasn't convinced about the plan, but as Naomi was so confident that it was a good idea I decided to go along with it.

I was late home because I had hockey practice. Craig was already in, which was a bit of a surprise. He seemed to be out so much of the time these days. I dumped my school bag and went over to the kettle.

'Where's Mum?'

'Getting changed from work,' he said gruffly. He was reading through the adverts in the local paper.

'What are you looking for?' I asked him.

'A job.'

I tried to speak calmly. 'Someone's going to find out about you bunking off school soon, you know, Craig.'

'Well, thank you for that, Detective Inspector Hannah McPherson,' he said.

Then Mum came in.

'Hello, Han. Good hockey?'

'It was OK.'

'Are you hungry?'

'Starving.'

'What about you, Craig? Are you hungry?'

'S'pose.'

Mum started cooking, while I went to get changed. As I came downstairs I could hear raised voices in the kitchen.

'Look, Craig, there's no point in denying it –'

It was Tony. I hadn't heard him arrive.

I crept down the last few stairs and sat down

on the bottom one to listen through the door again.

'I don't get why you'd rather believe Steve Woolman than me!' shouted Craig.

'For the simple reason that Steve was just making a passing comment. He doesn't have any axe to grind.'

'Well, it wasn't me he saw. Maybe he needs to get his eyes tested.'

'Now you're being stupid,' said Tony. 'Steve's seen you often enough up at football on Sundays. He knows exactly what you look like. So just tell me what you were doing hanging around town at ten o'clock in the morning when you should have been at school.'

'It was only once. I don't know why you're getting in such a sweat.'

'Ah! So you're admitting it!' Tony came straight back at him.

'I had to go into town to get a plastic folder thing for my history essay.'

'Oh come on, you can do better than that, Craig.'

'No, that's the best I can do,' Craig snarled. 'And as you're not my father, you can butt out.'

'You don't speak to Tony like that!' Mum suddenly said, not exactly loudly, just very firmly.

'Why not? *You* do,' Craig came back as fast as anything.

'That's nothing to do with you. Tony may not be your father, but he's been acting like it for the last five years. Just because he's moved out doesn't mean he doesn't care about you any longer.'

After that there was a silence. I wished I could have seen their faces. Mum had just made such a cool speech. Something really happy was bubbling about inside me because she'd defended Tony. I tried to make the bubble go away. I knew what happened when I dared to get my hopes up – they got knocked down again straight away.

I went into the kitchen a moment later, pretending I'd only just come downstairs.

'Oh hi, Tony!' I said.

'Hello, sunshine,' he said. 'What's new?'

They were pretending that everything was fine. The only giveaway was Craig, smouldering at the table, still flipping through the adverts, but smacking the pages down a bit harder now. I'd let him off the hook by coming in when I did. Come to think of it, I'd probably let Tony off the hook too. He must have known it wouldn't get him anywhere, yelling at Craig.

'Are you eating with us, Tony?' I asked, my voice coming out like an excited six year old's.

'No . . .'

'You can if you want,' said Mum.

Craig gave an exaggerated sigh and shook his head as though he could see right through Mum and Tony trying to act like reasonable people. Tony ignored him.

'No, it's all right . . .'

Then Craig got up and went out of the kitchen and Mum followed him, so Tony and I were left alone.

'I came round to chat with Mum about Craig, Han. He's been bunking off school.' I managed to look surprised. 'So, can you just give us a few minutes to talk to him about it in the other room?'

I nodded. 'I'll carry on with the cooking . . . Are you sure you can't stay?'

'No . . . I –'

'Are you eating round at Rachel's?'

'No . . .' He let out a light little laugh and put his hand on my shoulder. 'I don't spend my life round there, you know. It was just a coincidence that I happened to be there that evening when you came.'

I wanted to ask him why he couldn't stay and

eat with us then, but he'd already gone out. So the question stayed inside my head, joining the queue of all the other questions I never quite dared to ask.

10 THE ROCKET JOKE

I don't know what Tony and Mum said to Craig in the living-room yesterday evening. All I know is that today Craig came to school. I had to tell Naomi that the stalking plan was off. She was really disappointed. I think she was looking forward to the adventure. It's OK if it's not actually happening to you personally.

I saw Craig in the corridor with his mates. He was being the loudest of them all and he pretended not to see me. Katie and Naomi both gave me sympathetic looks.

'Ali Fairbarnes said *her* brother turned really

horrible when her parents separated,' said Naomi, tucking her arm through mine. 'Craig'll go back to normal soon, I expect.'

'Has your mum said anything to you about moving near your granny's?'

'No, and I keep crossing my fingers that she won't. The longer she doesn't mention it, the more hope there is that she'll change her mind.'

As we rounded the corner I got the shock of my life because there, coming out of the head teacher's office, was Mum.

'See you in history, then,' said Katie.

And Naomi mumbled something as they rushed off. It was obvious they were embarrassed. That was nothing to what *I* felt. I mean, having your mum in school is really bad news. And she'd only just missed bumping into Craig.

'Craig'll go mad if he sees you,' I whispered, grabbing her arm and pulling her down the corridor towards the nearest exit.

Mum smiled. 'He's just been in here with me. I want you to keep this completely to yourself, but he's agreed to see a counsellor.'

More questions joined the queue inside my head, but I just nodded and thought that at least I could strike one worry off my list, even if it was only a small one compared to the others.

But as the day went on I couldn't help thinking about what Mum had said. Surely if Craig was going to see a counsellor, she couldn't move away? The more I thought about it, the more I was certain I was right.

Until now I'd not had the courage to bring up anything to do with Mum moving. But now I felt so sure that everything was going to be all right, I couldn't keep quiet a second longer. At eight o'clock that evening I took a deep breath and spoke quickly before I could change my mind.

'Mum, you're not thinking of moving away, are you?'

She looked very taken aback. 'I –'

I interrupted quickly because I didn't want to hear any answer except 'No'. 'Well, now that Craig's seeing a counsellor you can't, can you? And he's got GCSEs and everything . . .'

I held my breath.

'Whatever made you think I was moving away?'

Now *I* must have looked taken aback. 'I – I heard you and Granny talking. Granny was answering you. She said something about how you'd be getting right away from Tony.'

Mum knitted her eyebrows together and a look of great concentration came over her face. Then after a few seconds she broke into a slow smile.

'Oh, *I* know what you're talking about! At one point, when I was really fed up, I jokingly said to Granny that I wished I could build a rocket and zoom off into outer space. And Granny wanted to make me feel better so she told me in a perfectly serious tone of voice that I'd certainly be getting right away from Tony if I did!'

The relief I felt was so great I would have broken into song if my mobile phone hadn't bleeped at that moment. It was a text message.

Hi Han, Got this mobile as early pres from Dad. U r my first text. Dad's JUST told me he FORGOT to give me your message about meeting up! REALLY sorry. Tomorrow? Same time and place? Love R

11 UNRAVELLING

I didn't tell my friends at school that I was going to meet Rachel. I was quite scared that she wouldn't be there again, and I'd feel a fool if I had to go back and tell them that. I knew it was stupid because after all, *she* was the one who'd text *me*, but I could still remember how I'd felt the last time I'd waited and waited.

I got there at ten to eleven. There was no sign of Rachel, but there was still time. By five to I was getting very anxious. All sorts of things went through my mind. Maybe she'd sent me the text message as a cruel joke, or maybe it wasn't from Rachel at all, but someone else playing an even crueller joke on me. By eleven o'clock it was obvious she wasn't coming. I felt so depressed, I could hardly raise the energy to walk away.

At five past the bell went. I checked my phone to see if Rachel had left me a message. She hadn't. So I switched it off. (If any mobile ever goes off in a lesson the phone is confiscated for the rest of the day. Who cares?)

Katie and Naomi had saved me a place in PSE.

'Where did *you* get to?' asked Naomi.

'I went to see if my sports shirt was in Lost Property and I had to wait ages for Mr Robinson to turn up with the key.'

'And was it?' asked Katie.

'Was it what?'

'Was it in Lost Property?'

'Oh . . . no.'

They both looked at me as though I was slightly mad.

I didn't take in a single thing all through PSE. I just kept wondering why Rachel had changed her mind – because there was no other explanation for her not turning up except that she'd changed her mind. I supposed there was a small chance that she might have been kept in all through break *and* had her mobile confiscated so she couldn't text to tell me, but it was pretty unlikely. For one thing, teachers hardly ever kept people in during break because it meant they had to miss their own break.

At the end of PSE Mrs Wild asked me to stay behind for a 'quick word'. I couldn't imagine what she wanted to say. I like Mrs Wild though, so I didn't mind. She's the teacher who you go to if you've got any problems. It's not her official job or anything, but because she teaches PSE, she's very popular. Katie and Naomi went on to save me a place in English.

'Chris Carter came to see me earlier today, Hannah. He seemed to think you might want to have a chat. And I must admit, I thought you seemed rather down just now,' she said when we were alone in the classroom.

I was amazed. I thought Chris was just a loud year nine boy. But he really cared.

'I'm OK,' I said, trying to smile because I didn't want to tell her why I was 'down' as she put it. It was too complicated and I couldn't be bothered.

'That's all right then, Hannah. Everyone has thoughtful days, after all.' She smiled. I don't know if she believed that I was OK, but she was nice enough not to push it. That's why everyone likes her. She's not nosy. She just seems to care about all the students. She was packing away her things slowly though, and I think that was to give me time to change my mind if I wanted to. I very nearly did, but I thought that if I started talking about how miserable I was, I might burst into tears, and the way I was feeling, I might not be able to stop. Not ever.

'Better get on to your next lesson then,' smiled Mrs Wild. 'Look, someone's here to collect you.'

I turned. There in the doorway stood Rachel.

I rushed over to her and she started gabbling as we walked along the corridor. 'I waited all break. I've just seen Katie and I asked her where you were. She said you'd been to Lost Property. Was it to pay me back that you didn't show up?'

'No . . . I was there. I waited there all break too. I don't get how come we missed each other. I made up the thing about Lost Property because I'd have felt so stupid telling Katie and Naomi that you didn't turn up – again.'

'Oh Han! Omigod! I'm so sorry. Where did you wait, exactly?'

'Behind the food technology block.'

'Dad said you said behind the canteen when you phoned him.'

'No, I never said that. I definitely said behind

the food technology block. I mean, why would I say the canteen?'

'I know, that's what I thought. But he said . . . he said . . .' She closed her eyes to concentrate. '*I* remember. He said, "She wants you to meet her in morning break behind the canteen, or whatever you call it nowadays." It never occurred to me that he thought the food technology block is just a modern name for a canteen!'

'So we've both been waiting for the whole of break –'

'I didn't dare text you, in case you were paying me back –'

We saw the funny side of it at exactly the same moment and cracked up. Then, being us, we both clicked that we were making too much noise, because the next lesson had already begun.

'SShhh!' we hissed at each other hysterically. And it's very painful being hysterical if you've got to be silent.

'Let's go to the loos,' I managed to splutter, giving Rachel a shove in the right direction.

Once we were there, we collapsed in another fit of giggles.

'My stomach's in agony,' said Rachel, bent over and clutching her middle.

'Mine too.'

Then gradually we stopped laughing and started talking. We completely skipped that lesson and neither of us cared at all. I reckoned that if the worst came to the worst I could easily go to Mrs Wild and explain.

So for half an hour we both told each other how terrible it had been without the other one, and we both said sorry at least a thousand times.

'Actually, it was partly my fault that Dad forgot to give me that message, because the moment he came off the phone from talking to you, I asked him what you wanted. He said you were worried about your mum finding out about the party. I felt so sorry for you because I'd already guessed you'd be worrying about that. I could just imagine that your mum would feel really gutted if she found out. I mean, those three all friendly together and her on her own after all these years. I felt more guilty than ever about arguing with you. So I told Dad it wasn't fair that you should have to worry about your mum, and I made him promise not to let her know he was organising the party with my mum. And after all that, I suppose the message went straight out of his head.'

So I had Rachel to thank for Tony keeping quiet. She was still being my friend even when we weren't speaking to each other.

I told her about Craig bunking off school, smoking and taking Mum's money. I wondered if she might already have heard about it from Tony, but she said that he hadn't mentioned it.

There was one thing I was dying to ask Rachel. 'So how come your mum and dad suddenly decided to make friends after all these years?'

'Because Mum phoned him up and said that I was in a terrible state and wouldn't tell anyone what was the matter.'

'And what *was* the matter?' I asked like a dur.

'That massive great argument with you, dumbo,' she said.

'Oh yeah – that day! It seems such a long time ago now.'

'I didn't mean to be horrible about your mum, honestly, Han. I just felt gutted because of everything. But I did listen to what you said about Dad and how your mum reckoned he didn't help enough and all that, and I've been dropping loads of hints about it, kind of hoping that he might turn up and do the odd job, or something. I don't know why I bothered actually. What's that saying? Oh yeah, it's like closing the stable door after the horse has bolted. I knew it was too late really.'

'Well, you did have some effect because he came round and stacked all the logs with me. Mum was amazed – and so happy, I could tell.'

I clutched Rachel's arm as we sat side by side with year seven coats hanging down from the pegs and draping all over us. 'I know it's stupid, but I even wondered whether there was a teeny chance that Mum and Tony might get back together again, especially now I know she's not planning on moving anywhere. I mean, they do seem to be getting on much better these days. I'm sure all their arguments came from Mum thinking Tony wasn't doing enough round the house, and he did the logs, didn't he, which must show that . . .'

Why was Rachel biting her lip and looking so serious? A shiver went through my body.

'What?' I asked in a whisper.

Rachel looked down.

'What?' I asked again.

'I think Dad's got a girlfriend,' came the reply.

The shiver made me freeze for a second.

'Why?'

'Partly because after he came round to our place that first time, Mum and Simon invited him two other times, but both times he said he'd already arranged something else.'

I felt the blood leave my face. There'd been that time when he was round at our place and Mum had invited him to stay and eat with us and he'd been cagey about why he couldn't. That would explain it . . .

'What's the other reason?' I asked flatly.

'I heard him talking with Simon that evening when he was round at our place, and they were deliberately keeping their voices down. Simon asked him something or other and Dad said, "She's called Tina. She works in Accounts." '

'But are you sure Simon was asking him who his girlfriend was?'

'No, but Dad looked all sort of . . . gooey.'

After a couple of minutes of silence while we both stared into space, wrapped up in our own thoughts, Rachel said, 'Do you want to see her?'

'What do you mean?'

'We could follow him from work and see where he goes.'

I couldn't bear the thought of Tony with someone else – especially not Tina from Accounts. I'd never met her, but I hated her. Right, I *would* see her. And I'd tell her exactly what I thought about her. I turned to Rachel.

'Yeah. This is what we do . . .'

12 OPERATION TINA

Rachel and I decided that the best bet was to go to school as usual in the morning so that we were there for registration, then sneak out at the end of the morning. We'd just have to risk one of the teachers noticing we were missing in the afternoon. Katie and Naomi knew what I was doing, so they could cover for me if a teacher asked where I was, and Rachel had got someone from her class to do the same. Ordinary subject teachers don't usually check up on things like dentists' appointments. They just take your word for it.

Tony's lunchtime is at one o'clock every day. He told me that ages ago. Now we were pretty sure that his girlfriend worked in the same firm as him, catching them together would be a whole lot easier. They were sure to spend their lunchtime together, weren't they?

So Rachel and I were all ready to leave school after the twelve-thirty bell. I was dreading seeing Tony with someone else and I think Rachel was very nervous about it too, but it was almost as though the dread was too great for us to manage, so we'd gone into a sort of mad mode, and everything suddenly seemed hysterically funny.

'Look casual,' I said to her out of the corner of my mouth, because she was walking across the car park like a bamboo cane. I probably didn't exactly look like the most laid back person in the world myself. 'Hang loose, Rach!'

We started strolling with loose legs and swinging bags.

'Do you think we might have gone a bit

too far the other way?' said Rachel.

'I'm just praying that no one's watching us.'

'Because, let's face it, we're rubbish at acting.'

We looked at each other and burst out laughing.

'Right, here goes!'

The next moment we were the other side of the school gate, hurrying down towards town. It started raining and neither of us had any way of keeping ourselves dry. It's sad wearing a coat at school and you definitely don't go round carrying an umbrella.

'Great!' I said despondently. 'We'll just have to run, because if we stop and shelter we'll be late for seeing Tony coming out of the office with Tina from Accounts.'

'I've got an idea . . .' said Rachel, puffing a bit because she hates running. 'Let's just call her Tina from now on.'

Of course in our hyper mood that struck us as amazingly funny. People who passed us stared at us as though we were demented – two sopping wet girls laughing their heads off. It was so lovely to be friends again – if only we weren't having to do such a horrible thing as follow Rachel's dad and my stepdad to try and see his girlfriend.

'We'd better try to blend in a bit more,' said Rachel, slowing down. 'Otherwise someone might report us to the head.'

By the time we got to the chemist across the road from Tony's office we were like drowned rats. We were also ten minutes early because we'd run so fast.

'At least we can shelter here,' I said, huddling up in the chemist's entrance.

But we couldn't even do that, because every time we pressed ourselves far enough back to get out of the rain, the stupid automatic doors opened. We kept on trying to judge it so we were out of the rain but not too close to the doors, by inching backwards in tiny shuffles. But the third time the doors opened the woman on the till did a shooing action with her hand.

'Let's watch out for Dad from inside,' suggested Rachel.

'I don't think the shop assistant will approve of that,' I pointed out.

So we went into the entrance of the shop next door and we'd no sooner got there than Tony appeared.

'There he is!' shrieked Rachel.

Unfortunately we'd missed the precise moment that Tony had come out of the building because we were too busy escaping the chemist's shop assistant. But he was walking purposefully along the road, umbrella up, and with a woman by his side who *only* had her hand tucked through his arm!

'That's got to be her!' said Rachel.

'We'll have to follow them,' I said.

'Don't you think we've got enough proof

now?' said Rachel, eyeing the spikes of rain that were attacking the pavement.

'I need more than proof. I want her to know exactly what I think of her.'

'OK.' (It doesn't take much to change Rachel's mind.)

So we hurried across the road and kept about twenty metres behind them for ages.

'Look at her legs,' Rachel whispered. She needn't have bothered about keeping her voice down. There was no way Tony could possibly have heard her even if she'd shouted, the noise from the rain and the traffic was so great.

'What about them?'

'They look kind of spindly. Your mum's legs are much better than that. Is Dad *blind*?'

'Nice coat though,' I commented, trying to be fair.

'Ugh! I don't think so.'

'Why not?'

'It's all wet.'

We cracked up again, and could hardly walk we were laughing so much.

'They've gone in to that pasta place! What do we do now, DCI Rach?'

'How much money have you got on you?'

I got my purse out of my school bag and counted. 'My bus fare plus one pound fifty-seven pence.'

'Well, I've got my bus fare plus eighty pence. Let's go in and have a drink each and some garlic bread or something, and walk home.'

'So we're not going back to school then?' I asked, because I suddenly realised we'd never actually discussed what we were going to do *after* Operation Tina.

'We can't really go back to school looking like this, can we?'

'No, that's true . . . but we can't go in the restaurant either. I mean, look at us! We'd wet the chairs and get chucked out.'

Another big snigger.

'And anyway, there's a pretty big chance that Dad and Tina'll notice us.'

I was determined now. 'Let's confront them!' I said (a bit dramatically, I admit).

'You're joking!'

'No! You know what grown-ups are like. They're on permanent guilt trips in case they've damaged their precious offspring. Tony'll take one look at us and blame himself for messing us up and making us do crazy things like follow him in the pouring rain without any coats.'

The more I thought about it, the more my brainwave seemed foolproof. Anyway I was still on a high. 'Come on, Rach. We've got to get rid of her. And think about it – we might get lunch as well.'

She looked a bit doubtful, but I was so full of confidence, I opened the restaurant door and went plunging in. In fact I was going so fast that I lost my footing on the slippery wet floor just inside, and collapsed in a heap on the floor.

Rachel gasped but it came out as more of a giggle than a gasp. 'Are you all right, Han?'

When I looked up the whole restaurant seemed to be staring at me.

Tony had just realised who it was causing the big stir.

'Omigod! Hannah!'

He came rushing over but I hardly gave him a second glance. My eyes were on the woman he'd left at the table. She was about twenty years older than him, with neat grey hair and a very smart suit. She was wearing half-glasses to study the menu. But over the top of them her eyes were looking at me with a mixture of concern and amusement.

I felt sick. As Tony heaved me to my feet, I only just stopped myself from saying, 'You're not going out with HER, are you?'

'Dad, the waitress wants to come past,' hissed Rachel.

She was right. Tony and I were blocking the

way and the waitress looked none too pleased.

'I don't know what you think you're doing, you two,' said Tony, suddenly turning stern as he pressed himself against the wall, yanking us both back with him, and apologising to the waitress at the same time. 'Come and sit at our table, then at least people'll stop staring at us.'

So we dripped our way across to Tony's table.

'This is Doreen,' said Tony. 'These are my daughters,' he told Doreen, rolling his eyes to the ceiling.

Doreen? Uh-oh! I think we'd made a bit of a mistake.

'I'm very pleased to meet you,' said Doreen primly. Then she took a proper look at the state of us. 'I hate to say this, but we're going to get thrown out if we're not careful. I suggest we go before that happens.'

'You're right,' said Tony. 'But I don't see why you should have your lunch hour ruined because of my daughters. You stay here, Doreen. I'll go and buy some sandwiches and take these two back to the office to dry off.'

'It's no problem! I don't really want to sit here on my own.'

She was *not* happy.

'Sorry,' Rachel and I said at exactly the same time.

That was like the magical turning point, because she suddenly broke into a big smile. 'Don't worry. It might have been an awfully long time ago, but I do remember what it's like being young and crazy.'

'Talking of which, I hope you've got a good explanation lined up for this behaviour,' said Tony, trying not to sound too cross in front of Doreen.

There was something about the way he spoke that brought me back to earth with a thud. I looked at Rachel and knew immediately that she was feeling the same. Every drop of hysteria had left my body. I felt like a nervous wreck.

We were going to Tony's office. We would finally meet Tina.

13 ACCOUNTS

The heat was the first thing that hit us when we got inside the office, then the smell.

'Freshly painted,' said Doreen as we marched through reception with our sandwiches.

The receptionist flashed us all big smiles. She must have been trained not to react, however strange the people coming through the door looked.

'With any luck somebody'll have a hairdryer,' said Doreen when we got to the top of the stairs. Rachel and I exchanged glances. *Even* more *chance of seeing Tina now.*

'I'll sort it out,' Doreen added.

'Thanks, Doreen. You're a gem,' said Tony. 'I'll be in here,' he added, pushing a door open.

'We'll try my room first,' said Doreen, pushing open another door and putting her head round.

It was frustrating that she was blocking our view. If the woman who'd taken Tony from my mum was in here, I wanted to see her. All I could do was listen to the conversation.

'I don't suppose any of you happens to have a hairdryer here, by any miracle?'

'Sorry. Try Accounts. They seem to keep spare tights and nail varnish and goodness knows what else in there. So why not a hairdryer?'

Rachel and I nudged each other as we followed Doreen to Accounts. My heart was beating hard. It had seemed like a joke when we were spying on Tony. But suddenly it wasn't funny any more. We were about to meet Tina – and I wasn't sure I wanted to.

Doreen opened a door and went inside. Rachel and I hovered in the doorway.

'Oh no!' whispered Rachel. 'There are so many of them.'

It was true. The room was huge and there were about twenty people in there. I did a quick count as Doreen talked to the woman at the nearest desk. Rachel must have been counting too.

'Seven men . . .'

'. . . and twelve women,' I finished.

'How are we going to find out which one's Tina?' whispered Rachel.

'We could just ask Doreen.'

'I never thought of that,' Rachel grinned.

'Hang on a sec – they've got little nameplate thingies on their desks.'

'OK, let's catch up with Doreen and follow her round.'

Doreen was asking the women one at a time because it would have been impossible to attract everyone's attention and ask them all at once, the noise of keyboards tapping and people talking on the phone was so loud. No one paid much attention to us. Some people didn't even notice us, and those who did hardly gave us a second glance.

When we caught up with Doreen she was at the desk of someone called Pat Thomas. I'd spotted the names Pauline Parker and Claire Evans on the way. None of the names at the next three desks was Tina's. We were rapidly narrowing it down. And no one had a hairdryer so far. I didn't care about that. I was only interested in the name. My blood was starting to boil, because Tina was sitting somewhere in this room typing away or chatting on the phone, happy as anything, while I was miserable because of her.

'What are we going to say when we meet her?' asked Rachel.

'I'm going to tell her I know all about her,

that she's ruining my life, that she's ugly compared to Mum – even if she isn't – and that Tony will soon get fed up with her, because he still loves my mum.'

Rachel was staring at me with big eyes. 'You wouldn't say all that in here?' she said a bit shakily.

'Just watch me!'

It was hard to see the last three nameplates because they were facing completely the wrong way. All three women looked up and smiled but the youngest one went straight back to her computer. I felt my heart beating harder as I wondered which one of these was Tina. It had to be one of them.

The young hard-working one was probably about twenty-five. She was very smartly dressed but not particularly good looking. The other two looked more glamorous and seemed much more interested in us. When Doreen asked about the hairdryer, the young woman just shook her head and said, 'Sorry', her eyes never leaving the computer screen.

'Workaholic!' mouthed the woman next to her, with a cheeky smile. The other one smiled at us as though we were slightly mad, but then reached into her drawer and took out a little portable hairdryer.

'You're in luck!' she said triumphantly. 'Da-da!'

'Hooray!' said Doreen, smiling at us two. 'Pity I didn't start at this end of the room! We'll be back with it in a few minutes if that's OK.'

'No problem.'

'Thanks, Rita.'

Rachel looked hacked off as we left the room because we still didn't know the names of two of the women. But I didn't care. We'd be back in there after a few minutes.

'One of them has got to be Tina,' hissed Rachel.

'We'll find out when we take the hairdryer back,' I hissed back.

'Good thinking, Han!'

Doreen showed us into a tiny room which looked like a general dumping room, and said she'd leave us to it.

'We'll give Rita her hairdryer back when we've finished,' I assured her.

'Right you are, girls . . . and you remember where your dad's office is?'

As soon as she'd gone Rachel turned to me with a hopeless look on her face.

'When we give the hairdryer back to Rita, we ask her which one is Tina,' I said firmly, in case she was thinking of chickening out.

Then I switched on the hairdryer and blasted my hair while I thought how much I hated this woman who sat there smugly in Accounts. I noticed Rachel was biting her lip as she watched me.

My legs felt shaky when we went back into the Accounts room. Rita spotted us walking over to her and gave us a thumbs-up.

'Thanks very much,' said Rachel, looking very nervous.

'Are you feeling better now you're a bit dryer?' Rita asked us with a grin.

'Yes, thanks.'

'Well, I know you're not Doreen's children, because they're grown-up . . .'

The woman at the next desk tuned in. She was obviously curious to find out who we were too. But the younger one just kept working away.

'We're Tony Simpson's daughters,' said Rachel.

And that was when the hard-working girl broke off what she was doing and said, 'Tony's daughters! I'm a big fan of your dad's!'

My heart was really racing. 'Are you Tina?'

'Yes, I am. How do you know my name? Has your dad mentioned me? That's amazing!'

She was so young. It was disgusting of her to go out with Tony. I fixed her with my coldest evil. She looked puzzled and blushed. Good, she was about to blush even more.

But before I could say a word, Rita said, 'Your dad gave Tina a reference for a new job, and she reckoned he must have said nice things about her, because she got the job.'

And all my angry words got stuck because my heart felt as though it had jumped into my mouth.

'I'm sure I'd never have got the job without his reference,' Tina was saying, looking less flustered. 'I'll be eternally grateful to him for that.'

'She's moving to Devon,' said Rita, 'where her boyfriend lives. That's why she's so happy.'

'And *we're* so sad,' said the third woman. 'Because she's a brilliant worker.'

Tina smiled and blushed. 'No, I'm not –'

'Yes, you are.'

'Anyway, I'd better get on,' said Tina, turning back to her computer.

'See!' said Rita and the other woman at the same time.

I stood there feeling about ten centimetres high. My whole body groaned. Tony was going out with Tina about as much as I was going out with Prince Charles.

We somehow managed to thank Rita again for the hairdryer and left the room.

'I feel so stupid,' Rachel said.

'Me too.'

14 ESTHER

We were in Tony's office. I felt as though I'd been called to see the head teacher for bad behaviour. Tony had asked us for an explanation. My mouth felt dry. All I could do was stare at the carpet. Rachel decided to come clean.

'It's my fault,' she said. 'I heard you talking about Tina from Accounts to Simon, and I . . . thought you might be . . . going out with her . . .'

Tony stared at us for about five seconds, then started talking in a really angry voice. 'So you hear me talking about someone, and that's it! Just like that, I'm going out with them! Why, Rachel? For God's sake tell me why? And then *please* tell me you haven't made a scene in there!'

He was pointing towards Accounts. His eyes were the wildest I'd ever seen them. When he's angry with Mum he's not like this – he's much more scornful looking.

Rachel and I shook our heads and Rachel said she was sorry. I could tell she was near to tears and it suddenly seemed unfair that she should be getting all the blame. I couldn't help what I said next.

'If you and Mum hadn't messed everything up in the first place, Rachel and I wouldn't be here now!'

The crossness kind of fell out of Tony's eyes as he looked down at the floor then back up to me.

'Yeah, OK, I deserved that,' he said quietly. 'Come on. I'm going to take you both back to school.'

* * *

At the end of school Rachel and I went to sit at the back of the bus. I got a shock when I looked down to the front.

'Rachel!' I squeaked. 'Have you seen who's sitting next to Craig?'

'Esther Black! Wow! People say she's going to get eleven A stars for GCSE.'

'I know, and if she's that brainy, what's she doing with my brother?'

Rachel giggled, 'Look, they're really deep in conversation . . . And did you see that smile he gave her?'

'Ssh! He'll hear you.'

'I don't think he'd hear a loudspeaker announcing the end of the world, if it was right next to his earhole. He's completely wrapped up in his conversation.'

'Yeah, but the incredible thing is, so is *she*!'

'I've been thinking about what happened in Dad's office,' said Rachel, suddenly looking serious. 'And I've realised something.' I was racking my brains to try and work out what she was going to say. 'The thing is, it's obvious Dad isn't going out with Tina . . . but he never said he wasn't going out with *anyone*. I think he's going out with someone else.'

'W-why?'

'Because why else would he have left your mum? Whenever anyone leaves anyone else on telly it's always because they've found someone new.'

A horrible wave of depression was coming over me with every word Rachel spoke. I was remembering the times when Tony said he wouldn't stay and eat with us.

'He always seems to have other arrangements doesn't he?'

Rachel nodded glumly. 'Like when Mum invited him to our place, but he couldn't come . . .'

We probably would have stayed like that – wrapped up in our hopeless thoughts – for the rest of the journey if Esther hadn't got up at that moment.

'Look! She's getting off here . . .' said Rachel.

'Omigod! She kissed him on the cheek. I'm going to faint!'

'They must be going out with each other!'

The next day at school, the first chance I got to talk to Rachel was at morning break. It was obvious she was desperate to tell me something. It was also obvious I wasn't going to like it.

'We all started talking about my disco last night,' she began in a rush, 'and Mum said that Uncle Keith was coming to it. So Susannah started counting how many adults were going to be there. She counted Mum, Dad, Simon and Uncle Keith. Then Mum said, "Actually, you can make that five because I think Dad's bringing a special guest. I straight away asked her who, and she looked serious and said I'd just have to wait and see." '

As Rachel was talking my body began to feel heavier and heavier. If only there was somewhere to sit down.

'So we were right,' I said weakly.

We were silent for a while, then Rachel said, 'My disco's not exactly going to be the best party in history, is it?'

I didn't know what to say. I'd be lying if I said I was looking forward to it. I was feeling more sorry than ever for Mum, because she'd be all alone while everyone, including Tony and his new woman, enjoyed themselves without her.

'I'm sure it'll be great,' I said, trying to look excited.

The next day I woke up feeling tense, but as the day wore on, as long as I didn't think about Tony, I found myself getting quite excited. I was going to wear my new tight shiny black cropped trousers and my turquoise top with black glitter on it. I'd got some silver earrings that hung down almost to my shoulders, and the first pair of high sandals Mum had ever let me have. The trousers and the earrings were the only things that were brand-new. In fact I hadn't even worn the trousers yet, so I couldn't wait. I tried on the whole outfit in the morning and went down to show Mum and Craig.

'You look gorgeous, love!' said Mum. Then she turned to Craig. 'Doesn't she?'

He shrugged. 'All right, I s'pose.'

'I don't mind running you down to Rachel's,' said Mum.

Rachel and I had arranged that I'd show up at her place around five o'clock so we could get changed together. Then at six-thirty we'd set off for the leisure centre. The guests were due to arrive at seven.

'It's OK, I'll walk,' I said quickly, because I was a bit anxious in case Tony was at Rachel's. Or worse still in case he was there with his girlfriend. I hated using that word about adults, but I couldn't think of a better one.

'It's pouring down,' said Mum. 'I'll take you.'

She sounded like she meant it.

'What are you going to do while I'm at the disco, Mum?'

'Oh, I'll be all right.'

'We'll look after her,' said Craig, coming through from the living-room where he and Esther had been watching telly.

I thought how different he looked these last few days. That heavy scowl had gone and so had his way of poking his head forwards. He was always smiling as though life was great.

'Can I see what you're going to wear?' Esther asked me.

We went up to my room together and I showed her my whole outfit on the hanger.

'It's beautiful,' she said, looking genuinely impressed. 'And I already know you look great in it because Craig's told me.'

'Craig actually gave me a compliment?' I couldn't believe my ears.

'Don't sound so surprised. He's always giving you compliments.'

'Not to my face. I thought he only just managed to put up with me.'

'You're joking! He thinks you're the best kind of sister. To try and quote his exact words, "You'd never know she was only thirteen. She doesn't moan, she doesn't pester me, she doesn't try to butt into my life, and best of all she doesn't judge me." '

'Oh!' That was all I could manage to say. My throat hurt too much for speaking at that moment. I'd never realised Craig thought all that about me.

15 THE MILLION DOLLAR
QUESTION

I was standing at Rachel's front door, waiting
for someone to answer my knock, and wishing
that Mum would drive off. Whenever she
dropped me anywhere she always waited to
check that someone was there before she
went. But just this once, surely she could go?
It was obvious there was someone here. Really,
I felt sure that Tony wouldn't be at Rachel's,
but I couldn't get this picture out of my head
of him answering the door all wreathed in
smiles with a beautiful woman right behind
him.

It was such a relief when Rachel appeared and gave my mum a big friendly wave then yanked me inside. Just before I shut the door I realised I hadn't actually waved to Mum myself. And now she was going off home all on her own.

'You've got to help me choose what to wear!' said Rachel dramatically, as I followed her upstairs. Every bit of carpet and bed in her room was covered with tops, trousers and dresses. I think she'd actually emptied out the entire contents of her wardrobe and all the drawers. Her hair was coated in some stuff that looked like glue.

'I'm trying out that conditioner again, even though I know it'll never work.'

'What about that blue top and those blue flares?' I quickly got back on the subject of clothes. 'That's what you said you were going to wear yesterday.'

'I know, but I don't look very nice in the

top. You can't wear a bra under it and I look completely flat without a bra.'

'Show me with and without, and let *me* decide.'

Three-quarters of an hour later we were still at it. It was between two pairs of trousers and two tops. In the end we decided which top went best with which trousers, then we tossed a coin for which outfit.

Rachel still wasn't convinced, but Simon had started yelling warnings up the stairs.

'Five minutes to go, Rach!'

'Three minutes to go and if you're not ready we'll go without you.' (Don't parents say ridiculous things – even step-parents!)

'OK, we're going *now*!'

So Rachel and I came clattering downstairs only to find that Tigs wasn't ready.

'Have you taken my new nail varnish, Rachel?'

'*Borrowed*, Mum. Only borrowed. It *is* my birthday.'

'No, it isn't. Not for two days.'

Eventually we all piled into the car.

'Are we meeting Tony there?' I whispered to Rachel.

'*Are* we, Mum?'

'I doubt he'll be there till gone seven.'

A horrible dull feeling came over me. Since I'd been at Rachel's I'd managed to put Tony out of my mind, but I couldn't any longer. It would be bad enough if he was there on his own, but this was going to be ten times worse.

The hall looked all bare and boring when we first got there and I could see the disappointment on Rachel's face. But the DJ, Pete Jawaski, turned up within minutes and by the time he'd got all his equipment set up and put the lights on, the place was transformed.

'Cool!' said Rachel, as we watched the lights chasing each other round the walls.

'Brand-new effect, this one!' said Pete, as a blue and silver silent firework seemed to go off right in the middle of the floor and then splash all over the ceiling and cascade down the walls.

'Wicked!' said Simon to Tigs, pretending to imitate us lot. 'Want a dance, babe?'

'I hope you're not going to embarrass me in front of all my friends,' said Rachel.

'That's my speciality!' he said, doing a really stupid dance, stabbing the air with his fingers like a madman.

'Rock on, man!' said Pete, turning the volume up. And that's when the guests started to arrive.

Rachel was busy unwrapping presents for the next twenty minutes, while Tigs and Simon finished off organising the food and drinks at the far end of the hall. My present was hidden under Pete's table. I was saving it for later when Tony walked in with *her*. I wanted something to be doing when the awful moment arrived.

The trouble was, all Rachel's friends had

arrived and given their presents. Even Uncle Keith had turned up clutching a great big teddy bear.

'I don't have a clue what thirteen-year-olds like – so I thought I'd get you this, because you liked the one I got you when you were four.'

Everyone laughed. Rachel loved it. She'd chucked out all her teddies and dolls and things last year and I knew she was quite sad that she hadn't just kept one teddy or something.

So now it was my turn. I couldn't put it off any longer. She opened my carefully wrapped present and her eyes lit up at the sight of the hair straightener.

'Thanks, Han!' She gave me a big hug, and seeing my anxious face, whispered, 'Forget about him. It'll be fine. Come on, let's dance.'

So I tried to dance because everyone else was. Even Simon, Keith and Tigs in a little group. But my heart wasn't in it. Then one of Rachel's friends said something that gave me a shock.

'Here's your brother and his girlfriend, Hannah!'

Craig! And Esther! What were they doing here?

'I invited them,' said Tigs, flashing me a smile.

'I didn't tell you because I thought it would be a nice surprise,' said Rachel, looking pleased with herself.

'Hiya!' called Craig with a grin. Esther gave a little wave then they held hands and walked over to chat to the DJ.

At that moment I happened to catch sight of Rachel's face. She'd stopped dancing and was staring as though she'd seen a ghost.

'What?' I asked as I turned to see what was fazing her like that.

Then I got the biggest shock of my life. Mum and Tony had just walked in. Tony had his arm round Mum's shoulder. My body felt as though it was full of heat waves pushing their way out.

'What are *they* doing here?' asked Rachel in a faint voice.

I just stared. Neither of them had spotted me.

Tigs appeared beside Rachel and me. I felt as though I was in the middle of a nightmare. Any second now she'd see who Tony had brought with him and she'd go absolutely mad. My heart nearly stopped when I saw her look over to the door. Then it nearly stopped again because I couldn't believe what I was hearing.

'Oh good,' she said, putting her hand on her cheek nervously. 'Tony managed to persuade your mum to come. I was so hoping he would. Isn't it great?'

She was smiling at Rachel and me as though she'd just taken our blindfolds off and we'd found ourselves in Disneyland.

'B-but . . . w-why?' I managed to utter.

'Because I thought it was time we adults all started acting our age,' she said, winking at me.

'Except for Uncle Keith, of course, who's a hopeless case and will always continue to act his shoe size, I fear!' She put a hand on my back and gave me a little push, then her voice softened. 'Go and say hello then, love.'

So I walked shakily over to Mum and Tony. The whole room was buzzing and sparkling. All around us people were flinging their arms around dancing to the loud music as the lights whirled and flashed. Just the three of us were completely still. Then Mum put her arm round me.

'All right, Han?'

I nodded, feeling a lump in my throat. 'I didn't know you were coming.'

'It was only decided at the last minute.'

'No it wasn't,' said Tony. 'I decided days ago. I've just been plucking up the courage to ask you. I felt like I did when I was about sixteen, asking my first girlfriend on a date!'

I searched Mum's face. 'I don't understand. I

thought – I mean, I never thought you'd come to a place where . . .'

It was as though everything round me was so fragile that if I said the wrong thing I might break it.

'Your mum and I have decided it's only fair that we try and tell you what's been happening,' said Tony. He looked at Mum and she carried on.

'It's all been my fault –'

'No, it hasn't,' said Tony.

'Well, yes, it has,' Mum insisted.

Then they both laughed. 'Let's not argue about that!' said Tony.

'OK,' Mum went on. 'You know that we've always had this huge rift between Rachel's family and ours? Well, Tony finally couldn't put up with it any longer. We were arguing more and more and I refused to change anything, so Tony left. That's it in a nutshell.'

'Except that the moment I'd gone, I regretted

it,' said Tony. 'Only I knew something had to change or we'd always be stuck in the middle of this ridiculous war.'

I felt as though my brain was full of bits of a puzzle that I had to piece together to make any sense. 'So, you weren't arguing because Tony didn't help enough round the house?'

Mum looked at me blankly. 'No.'

'And you didn't have a girlfriend, Tony?'

Tony sighed and gave me a sort of half-smile. 'I thought we'd already dealt with that one.'

'I mean *another* one, not Tina.'

'Tina? Who's she?' asked Mum.

'A woman at work. I'm afraid Hannah's and Rachel's imaginations have been working overtime.'

Mum laughed and the laugh turned into a really special smile for Tony. He kissed her cheek quickly, then grabbed her hand. *And* mine.

'Come on, you lot. Let's have a dance.'

'Hang on!' said Mum. 'I haven't said Happy Birthday to Rachel yet.'

She went over to Rachel and give her a tiny present that she took out of her pocket. Rachel opened it quickly then kissed Mum. I could see her eyes shining in the light, and then I saw this beautiful silver chain that Rachel was holding up. All her friends swooped on it to look more closely.

Then *my* eyes came out on stalks because Mum went over to Simon, Tigs and Uncle Keith. It was incredible to see Mum and Tigs talking to each other after all these years. It was as though an enormous iron had appeared and settled on the hall, ironing away all the problems and jealousies.

I was desperate to ask Tony the million dollar question, but I was too scared of the answer.

'Are you – does this mean – will you be coming back to live with us now?'

He was wearing a sort of sad smile and still

looking over at Mum. 'We'll see, love. We'll see. First things first, eh?'

I nodded and gave him a big hug, feeling a little bubble of happiness somewhere deep inside me. I thought this one was different from the others I'd felt – somehow stronger, less easy to burst. Then I saw Mum coming back.

'I'll go and dance with Uncle Keith, I think,' I said to Tony, because I wanted to leave Mum and him alone and it was the first thing that came into my head. 'He doesn't half look stupid trying to butt in on Simon and Tigs.'

Tony grinned. 'You wouldn't dare!'

'Just watch me!' But Tony knew me well. I wasn't sure that I *did* dare.

Rachel grabbed me as I headed vaguely in Uncle Keith's direction. 'I'm so happy, Han. I'm sure it's all going to be OK now. Dad looks desperate to get back with your mum, doesn't he? I was thinking, we ought to have another go at Mission Unite to help him.'

I suddenly remembered what Esther said about one of the reasons Craig thought I was such a great sister – *She doesn't try to butt into my life . . .*

'No, let's leave them alone to sort it out for themselves.'

Rachel frowned, then grinned as she looked over my shoulder. I followed her gaze. Mum and Tony were clutching each other like a couple of teenagers as they danced. 'Good thinking, Han!'

'Uncle Keith,' I called, just loudly enough for Tony to hear. 'Want a dance?'

'You bet I do!' he replied.

And over Mum's shoulder Tony gave me a big thumbs-up sign.

Step-Chain

DON'T TELL MUM

1 SEARCHING FOR THE BUZZ

I was walking into town at the end of another scintillating day at school, and talking to myself, like you do. Well, *I* do, anyway. I know some people think I'm completely barmy, but then I'm sure there must be others who think it's all part of my endearing character. I don't care what anyone thinks at the moment, because I've got to keep gabbling away to sort things out.

It's not fair. I mean, of all the people in the world, how come *I'm* the one to be staggering around under these mega great mountains of pressure? I mean, all I want is one little Coke in Ricoco's café, so I can suss out this boy who works there. My best friend, Claire, has been on about him for days.

'You're going to absolutely love him,' she keeps telling me at school. 'He's soooooo good looking.'

'So why don't *you* fancy him then?' I wanted to know.

'Because he's not my type. He's too nice and neat and normal . . . and he goes red easily.'

And that's when I realised that he probably wasn't that good looking at all. Claire's just desperate for me to fancy *someone – anyone –* so we'll both be in the same boat. I've never fancied any ordinary people – only pop stars, whereas Claire's spent the last year fancying one boy after another. At the moment it's the boy who works on the checkout at the supermarket. She keeps telling me what a great feeling it is. 'Your whole body buzzes like crazy, Beth!' I keep wondering when *my* body might show some sign of buzzing like crazy, but so far, no luck.

Back to the mega tonnes of pressure. Last night Anne, my stepmother – and don't get me wrong, I love her dearly – said I was to come straight home after school because (1) I haven't got any money (that's true), (2) I'm behind with my homework (also sadly true) and (3) I'm doing far too much gadding about these days. Now that last one is blatantly untrue. At least, *I* think it is. It would help if I knew what 'gadding' meant, but I'm pretty sure I haven't been doing it.

Anyway, after Anne had passed sentence on the Coke at the café, I went to a great deal of trouble phoning Claire and whispering down the phone that she had to ring me back a subtle twenty minutes later, to remind me about a very important 'netball practice'. So far, so good. Or at least that's what I thought. But, stupidly, I hadn't taken into account that my adorable little stepbrother, Jon, might happen to be loitering outside my bedroom with his ear pressed to the door.

So when I came to tell Anne twenty minutes later that Claire had just phoned me and, silly me, I'd completely forgotten about the netball practice after school the next day, the earwig pipes up, 'She hasn't got a netball practice, 'cos I know.'

'I *have*!' I screeched, which was overdoing it slightly, I admit.

'She's just made it up so she can go to Ricoco's,' Jon informed Anne.

I resisted the urge to strangle him – some kind person really should have done that long ago to put the rest of us out of our misery – and told Anne that I was Goal Attack and they couldn't do without me. I trailed off into some sort of pleading jargon that covers all occasions when I'm desperate to get the parental OK as quickly as possible, then get off the subject.

'You know I don't mind you staying for netball practice, Bethany,' came the verdict, 'but I've already told you you're not to go to the café, and I'm trusting you not to.'

Uh-oh! Tough one. Anne knows exactly how to get me where it hurts. So there I was, stranded on the horns of a dilemma, which is as painful as it sounds, believe me.

But to make matters worse, Jon went ominously quiet after Anne had spoken, and right now I'm fearing the worst. So while I'm walking along talking to myself, I'm looking to the right and left, because something tells me that any minute now, smart-kid Jon is suddenly going to catch me out. I know exactly how his evil little mind works. First he will have got himself an invite to his friend Alex's house after school. Then he'll probably get Alex to cover for him while he nips down to the bottom of his garden, climbs over the wall, runs down the alleyway, and, hey presto(!), into the high street.

And guess where I am right now? Yep. The high street.

And what do you know? There he is! Grinning his stupid head off.

'What are *you* doing?' I snapped.

In my heart I knew I was on to a loser from the very start, but there was just one chance. I looked around for any sign of Alex's mum. Good, she was nowhere to be seen. I narrowed my eyes and spoke in my most teacherly voice. 'You'd better not be on your own or I'll tell Anne.'

I was kind of hoping MI5 boy's grin might disappear at the sound of those foreboding words. But no chance.

'You can tell Mum what you like, she won't be interested, because Alex's mum is only back there . . .' He flapped his hand behind him. I had no way of knowing if he was telling the truth or not, and no time to find out because he was going in for the kill. 'And

I reckon Mum'll be more interested in what *I* tell her about you not being at netball.'

I so wished he wouldn't do that 'I' thing, where his voice goes all loud and clever.

'For all you know I might be just buying something like . . . a snack . . . for the netball practice . . .'

Well, those words had to be in with a chance of winning the most-stupid-excuse-of-the-year trophy.

'You're going to Ricoco's. It's obvious,' he grinned. 'I won't tell Mum if you give me a pound. And I know you've got a pound because I saw it in your room.'

He also knew he'd got me cornered. And what's more, he knew *I* knew he'd got me. I decided not to waste any more time on the nauseating, grinning little tale-telling, blackmailing MI5 earwig.

'I'll give it to you at the weekend. I can't go into Ric's with no money, can I?'

'It'll be *two* pounds at the weekend.'

My jaw was hanging open. I'd never imagined that Jon could be this mercenary. 'Who put you up to that? Best friend Alex?'

He shook his head violently. Good, he was acting a bit more like a ten-year-old now.

'Alex'd never say anything like that. Alex likes you. In fact –' the smile turned into an embarrassed giggle – 'he fancies you.'

I rolled my eyes to the sky, and spoke in a withering voice. 'Alex is nine, yes?' He nodded. 'And I'm thirteen going on fourteen, if you remember.'

I gave him a look that was supposed to show I was about as impressed by his latest revelation as I was by the fact that caterpillars eat leaves. Then I deliberately changed it into a deeply disappointed look, and spoke in a matching voice to try and make the evil little blackmailer crack.

'I can't believe that I've got such a horrible

brother.' And with these words I reached into my pocket and held out the pound coin.

This was a big gamble. I was playing the guilt card, and it seemed to be working pretty well. He began to squirm as he looked at the coin.

'You can give me two at the weekend – I've told you.'

'I can't afford two. Take this one. I'll just have to have a few sips of Claire's Coke, that's all.'

'Where *is* Claire?' he asked, looking round.

'She's meeting me in there. She had to nip home for something first.'

The grin came back. 'I bet *I* know why. It's to get changed, isn't it? She's got a boyfriend, hasn't she? She wants to look all –'

He broke off abruptly, because guess who'd suddenly appeared? Claire. She was wearing hipster jeans, a tight black top and a denim jacket. Her long light brown hair hung exactly where it was supposed to hang, and she looked altogether brilliant. Standing next to her in my school uniform, I felt like a pathetic little girl.

Claire looked at the pound I was holding out. 'What's happening?' she asked brightly.

'Ask him,' I said, jerking my head in Jon's direction, feeling a little flutter of hope. Jon wouldn't want to show his horrible greed in front of my sophisticated friend with the shining hair, would he?

'Bethany owes me,' he tried to explain.

'Is that your last quid, Beth?'

I sighed and nodded.

'You'll have to pay him later,' said Claire. 'We need that quid for Ric's. I haven't got any money at all.' She turned to Jon as she dragged me away from him. 'See ya.' Then she broke into an awkward run, still clutching me and my pound. 'He's *soooo* gorgeous, Beth!'

I turned my head sharply, because my mind was still on my stepbrother, and I thought Claire must have suddenly lost her marbles.

'The waiter at Ric's,' she explained, her eyes going gooey. 'Though not as nice as the boy at the supermarket,' she added.

Then we were there. At the café.

Collect the links in the step-chain ...

1. To see her dad, Sarah has to stay with the woman who wrecked her family. Will she do it? Find out in *One Mum Too Many!*

2. Ollie thinks a holiday with girls will be a nightmare. And it is, because he's fallen for his stepsister. Can it get any worse? Find out in *You Can't Fancy Your Stepsister*

3. Lissie's half-sister is a spoilt brat, but her mum thinks she's adorable. Can Lissie make her see what's really going on? Find out in *She's No Angel*

 4. Becca's mum describes her boyfriend's daughter as perfect in every way. Can Becca bear to meet her? Find out in *Too Good To Be True*

 5. Ed's stepsisters are getting seriously on his nerves. Should he go and live with his mum? Find out in *Get Me Out Of Here*

 7. When Bethany discovers the truth about Robby, she knows her family will go ballistic. Is it possible to keep his secret from them? Find out in *Don't Tell Mum*